Sabina
and the
Mystery of the Ogre

Christopher Okemwa

First Edition: August 2015
Published by Nsemia Inc. Publishers (www.nsemia.com)

Edited By: Matunda Nyanchama
Cover Concept & Illustration: Abel Murumba
Cover Design: Danielle Pitt
Layout Design: Kemunto Matunda

Note for Librarians:
A cataloguing record for this book is available from
Kenya National Library Services.

ISBN: 978-9966-082-07-7

Acknowledgement

The Burt Award for African Literature recognizes excellence in young adult fiction from African countries. It supports the writing and publication of high quality, culturally relevant books and ensures their distribution to schools and libraries to help develop young people's literacy skills and foster their love for reading. The Burt Award is generously sponsored by a Canadian philanthropist, Bill Burt, and is part of the ongoing literacy programs of the National Book Development Council of Kenya, and CODE, a Canadian NGO supporting development through education for over 50 years.

FOREWORD

The National Book Development Council of Kenya (NBDCK) is a Kenyan nongovernment organization made up of stakeholders from the book and education sectors. It promotes the love of reading, the importance of books and the importance of quality education.

The Burt Award for African Literature project involves identification, development and distribution of quality story books targeting the youth, and awarding the authors. It is funded by Bill Burt, a Canadian philanthropist, and implemented by the NBDCK in partnership with the Canadian Organization for Development through Education (CODE).

The purpose of the Burt Award books such as *Sabina and the Mystery of the Ogre* is to give the reader high quality, engaging and enjoyable books whose content and setting are portrayed in an environment readers can easily identify with. This sharpens their English language and comprehension skills leading to a better understanding of the other subjects.

My profound gratitude goes to Bill Burt who, through CODE, accepted to sponsor the Burt Award for African Literature in Kenya. Special thanks also go to the panel of judges for their dedicated professional input into this project. Finally, this foreword would be incomplete without recognizing the important role played by all NBDCK stakeholders whose continued support and involvement in the running of the organization has ensured the success of this project.

Ruth K. Odondi
Chief Executive Officer
National Book Development Council of Kenya

The Clash!

Sabina's mother swung through the door with the fury of a woman, scorned. She had suffered many days of excruciating ridicule. Sarcastically referred to as a mother of *egesagane,* an uncircumcised girl, she had endured torment and distress in the village. She had undergone torture and utmost pain.

"Mother of *egesagane!*" women would speak behind her back.

"Mother of a cowardly girl!" men would mock her.

"Mother of a dirty girl!" young girls would shout at her and run away to hide in the bush, as if teasing her.

Now, as she crossed the door-way into her daughter's hut, she swore never to allow this disgrace to continue in her life. With flaming cheeks, she stopped in the middle of the room, crushed and degraded.

"Sabina! Sabina!" she shouted.

"Yes, Ma," Sabina answered as she came out of her bedroom.

"Have you prepared yourself?" she asked.

"No, Ma"

"Be quick. You should join other girls at Lokolo-kolo's house?"

"Ma—," Sabina started up, then caught her breath.

"What?" her mother barked. "I don't want to hear any of your excuses. Dress up and join other girls at Lokolo-kolo's. There you will be prepared for the *night of the ogre* that is coming tonight. You should not miss it. It is a ritual you have to undergo before the *day of the ogre*—the day of the knife! As a brave girl, you should look forward to these two important occasions," she explained. "The night of the ogre is scheduled to come tonight. Hurry up! You should be there this morning to be counselled, guided and motivated. After the night of the ogre, you will come home tomorrow morning and we shall prepare you for the day of the ogre when you will receive the cut."

"But Ma—"

"Don't tell me!" she shouted her down, throwing up her hands in utter frustration. "Look at yourself!" she sneered. "You are now fifteen years, an old mama! Your *titis* stand huge on your chest; soon you are getting married. Do you want to be married with your dirty *gento?"*

"Ma, I am still young, I have not even started thinking about marriage."

"Don't talk back to me!" the mother roared. "Your age mates are already cut. They were circumcised last year. Some intelligent ones are already attracting men to marry them. Last year you evaded the cut by feigning sickness. We thought you were too sick to face the ogre. We decided that, since you were sick, there was no harm if you did it a year later. This is the year. Whether you like it or not, you must be cut. Even if you are dying in your bed, or you are dead, we shall still cut your corpse this time round!"

"No, Ma," Sabina pleaded. "The cut? Oh no! I don't want to undergo the cut, Ma."

"What? Why? You don't want to undergo the cut? Is that what you say?" the mother shouted, her voice shaded in anger.

"The cut, Ma, has no meaning," Sabina sobbed. "I want to remain as I am now."

"Remain uncut? At your age? Who will pay dowry for an unclean dirty fool?"

"I can do it next year, Ma!"

"Next year?" her mother's face fumed with anger. "Do you know the humiliation your father and I are undergoing? Do you know? Silly girl!"

"But Ma—"

"Fool! I can't even sit with other women because they see me as a mother of a dirty girl? And your father? — a father of an old, grey-haired girl! Is that the torture you want to subject your parents to? Sabina, it is time you saved our family's image! It is time you took away this pain and torture."

"I don't think I want to be circumcised, Ma."

"Sabina, what are you saying?" the mother cried out. She suddenly moved forward, swung her right arm backwards and slapped Sabina across the cheek. The slap reeled Sabina down to the floor and she fell with a thud. She curled herself on the floor and covered her face, sobbing.

"That serves you right," her mother growled. She then took Sabina by the scruff of her neck, brought her to her feet and pushed her into her bedroom. "Prepare yourself now, silly girl! I want to see you leaving for Lokolo-kolo's house, now!"

Shaking with fury, the mother left the hut.

Preparations

Sabina walked meditatively along the narrow path that was paved with shrubs and thick undergrowth. Scattered chrysanthemums, ferns and wild flowers intermingled with the shrubs, producing colour and splendour in the gentle morning sun. After half an hour of walking, the footpath entered into a dark forest of thick woods whose canopy blocked the sun, allowing it to reach the forest floor in little trembling triangles and squares. Birds twittered and chirped excitedly, complementing the wind's wailing orchestra. The path became indistinct from time to time and she had to wade through clusters of dry leaves and broken twigs to find the path again.

She crossed a thorny fence that ran across the plain field. She then entered another open space with scattered chrysanthemums. The landscape descended and ahead was a stream. She stood at the bank of the stream and peered ahead. She listened: noises, chattering and laughter. These were other girls who had arrived at Lokolo-kolo's homestead. Was it excitement, or a cry of horror, she wondered. What were the feelings of those little girls? Were they not afraid or terrified like she was? She was suddenly filled with fear and a tremble came upon her little lips. She would be in the homestead in a moment.

She walked through a wooden gate that swung on creaking hinges. The home had two houses, both built of grass thatch, sticks, mud and cow dung. A belt of white clay ran at the lower part of the walls. Attached to the bigger of the two huts was a chicken shed made of old corrugated iron sheets. There were many chicken in it. Sabina also noticed that Lokolo-kolo also kept many cats and ducks that cluttered the whole ground. Sabina had been told that Lokolo-kolo lived alone without children or grandchildren. No one ever explained why she lived by herself. Sabina also did not know whether Lokolo-kolo ever had children or ever got married. Many people said that she led a mysterious life.

Sabina went past the bigger hut and headed towards the second one in which the little girls congregated. The girls inside craned their necks through the bamboo window to welcome their *kegori, age mate*. Sabina squirmed and felt blood recede from her dark face. Her cheeks flamed as she entered the hut through a bamboo, dung-smeared door. All eyes turned on her.

She quickly threw herself onto a traditional three-legged stool that was near the door. There were twelve girls seated in the hut. The inside walls of the hut were decorated with clay, dung and beads. Two curved horns were stuck in the clay walls on both sides of the entrance into the inner room. Beads fixed onto a string ran down both sides of the entrance. Flowers in pots stood at one corner and in the other were a drum, a big milk gourd and a basket made of twigs. Fixed on the walls were old faded photos of past age sets who had taken training with Lokolo-kolo. The ceiling was made of mat and rafters that ran across the loft. Cobwebs hung down from the old badly-fixed mat like black confetti.

While Sabina sat forlornly alone, loud laughter came from the group of girls seated at the corner. She looked towards them. They were talking in low tones then looking towards her, and bursting into laughter from time to time.

"Omong'ina! An old woman!" they were heard saying, and this sent a cold chill down Sabina's back. *"Omong'ina!"* their voices became louder, punctuated with laughter and giggles. As they talked, they kept turning their heads towards Sabina. Some sneered and spat on the floor while others showed remorse and sympathy on their faces. Sabina smelt a rat. She sat gazing at the ground.

Suddenly one girl stood up and walked towards her. The girl sat next on an empty stool next to her. The girl glanced up at Sabina with mingled suspicion and mockery: "Are you of our age-set? Tell me?" she asked, rather impatiently. "How old are you? Are you thirteen like us?"

Sabina didn't answer any of the questions. She just looked on with a blank face, wordless. The other girls at the corner exhibited restlessness and impatience. They turned fully towards Sabina and burst into laughter again.

"Omong'ina! omong'ina!" they whispered, murmuring, laughing and slapping their hands together. Some laughed until torrential tears flowed down their cheeks.

"Are you of our age set?" the girl continued with her nagging commands. A second girl sprang up from the corner and joined them.

"Tell us, are you of our age set?" the first girl insisted. Sabina glanced down at the floor and refused to talk. "We have been told that you were meant to go in for the ogre last year or the year before last year. Is that true?" she asked and looked at Sabina fully in the face. "Tell us!" she commanded. Sabina did not open her mouth. "You are two years older than any of us. Isn't it true? Tell us," the girl insisted, but Sabina did not part her lips in talking.

"You were meant to go in for the ogre last year with my sister, Moraa, or the year before last year, with my elder sister, Nyamoita!" the second girl squealed, sneered and exulted. "What are you doing here among your 'grandchildren'?" She asked, so mockingly and loudly that all the girls in the room heard her and burst into laughter. They laughed, laughed and slapped their thighs. Their faces were wet with tears, their noses ran with mucus. They wiped their faces and blew their noses. Sabina's body was lashed with a whip of humiliation. Her heart was filled with acute pain that found no relief in tears. She lowered her head and burst into a sob. The room quietened.

Suddenly a figure appeared at the door: a thin, tall, wild-eyed woman with foaming lips. The girls quickly sat up straight on their stools. The woman, wrapped in a red scarf, inquisitively swept her eyes across the room. Sabina raised her head and stole a quick glance at the woman and dropped her head. When she raised it a few seconds later she was met with an inquisitive stare: "Sabina!"

"*Eee Magokoro,*" she mumbled confusedly and quickly stood up, her eyes fixed on the floor. All the eyes were on her. Murmurs, whispers and grumbles filled the house. Sabina was bathed in sweat.

"So you have come?" the old woman asked.

"Yes, *Magokoro,*" she said and sketched a line on the floor with her toe, while her mouth suckled on the index finger of her right hand.

"Why didn't you come in the morning?" the woman asked. "The day is almost over. You have missed a lot of good lessons we have had since morning," she said and the whole room was abuzz with murmurs; some girls were grinning while others were sneering in Sabina's direction.

Sabina was tense. She continued gazing at the floor, and her tiny eyes grew dark with humiliation. She raised her head and started to say: "My Pa and Ma__" then suddenly stopped. Her tongue was heavy as a lump of saltfish in her mouth, moving against the words she wanted to make. She wrung her fingers and twiddled with the hem of her pullover. Her big toe curved itself into a hook and quickly sketched a triangle, a square and a zero on the earthen floor __ and quickly rubbed them all at once.

"Come here!" Lokolo-kolo's voice boomed. Sabina quickly raised her head, squirmed towards the elderly woman, bowed, and clutched the withered, vein-lined hand that felt like a stick—such that one could cook with it! "You should have come in the morning," Lokolo-kolo said, her wild eyes piercing Sabina. "You hear?"

"Yes, *Magokoro*," Sabina said and quickly drew letter O on the floor.

"Last year you were sick," Lokolo-kolo explained. "The year before last year, you hid yourself for two weeks until the ogre season was over. What about this year? Are you prepared for the ogre?" Lokolo-kolo asked in a matter-of-fact way, sending the entire pack of girls in the house into a roar of laughter. They laughed and cried with derision. Some clapped their hands jeeringly while others made faces of scorn at Sabina.

"Omong'ina!" a muffled voice was overheard above the din of the laughter. Lokolo-kolo quickly looked in the direction where the word came from. Her eyes turned wild and her nostrils grew huge and quavered.

"Bad manners!" Lokolo-kolo uttered with fury, her lips foaming and her nostrils trembling. She turned to Sabina and asked again: "So, now, tell me, my over-age girl. Are you prepared for the ogre this year?" There was loud silence in the room. The girls exchanged curious glances, their faces looking like they would burst any time. Heads turned, eyes darted around the house and gestures of mischief filled the house.

"No, yes, no, sorry!" Sabina stammered, confused, bewildered.

"No-o-o-o-o?" Lokolo-kolo shouted, prolonging the question, opening her eyes wide in surprise. The girls could not hold up any longer and finally burst out into squeals of laughter. Sabina cringed in terror. The ground underneath her feet swayed, and the room was filled with darkness.

"Yes, I am ready, *Magokoro*," she fumbled for the words, her tiny eyes piercing the earthen floor.

"Okay, you can sit now."

Sabina released the old lady's hand. She choked and trembled as she turned round to look for her stool. She sat quickly and quietly.

The girls turned their eyes to Lokolo-kolo and paid attention to what she was saying.

"Omong'ina!" the term etched itself in Sabina's mind. She hated the girls, she hated Lokolo-kolo, she hated herself and she hated her community. She tried to forget and concentrate, but the term dug deep into her mind, planted itself there and grew exuberantly into a huge plant. She felt a snake of humiliation go down her back over and over again.

"You will spend a full day here!" Lokolo-kolo suddenly burst out with a tone of urgency. "Today we have the night of the ogre as you know. The night is simply here with us. You've got to be prepared. You should know that you are soon becoming women, and not the little girls that you are. And today's session is the way to go." She moistened her foaming lips, revealing a dark tongue that protruded from her tiny severe mouth like a black serpent.

The night of the ogre! Sabina thought and a lump closed her throat in panic. The word "ogre!" etched itself in her mind. The two images, *ogre* and *omong'ina,* crisscrossed her mind like giant monsters, threatening to kill her. They referred to her as *omong'ina,* an old woman. Then the ogre!—a beast that will come tonight to swallow them all.

After Lokolo-kolo's speech, the girls went out for a break after which lunch was brought in. The women who prepared lunch at Lokolo-kolo's main hut brought it in trays made of sticks, sisal strings and dry cow-dung. They served the *ugali* and sweet potatoes in *ekee* and porridge in calabashes. The girls sat outside under a tree and ate their lunch amid anxiety and tension.

After lunch the girls assembled in the hut. Lokolo-kolo continued with her speech about the night of the ogre: "Tonight is the night of the ogre. It is the night we are all waiting for with bated breath. The hour is finally coming! You will be swallowed by the ogre. The ogre will take you to the sea, carrying you in his stomach. There, in the sea, you will be able to eat fish and other animals," she clarified. Sabina was filled with horror. A thin layer of sweat enveloped her skin. She took in a deep breath and let it out with terror. "You should remember to take razor blades with you, to cut the intestines, kidneys, livers and gizzards inside the ogre's stomach and bring them home for your siblings and parents. They are very sweet parts," she added and her nostrils trembled, widening into a pair of whistles. "The ogre is a huge monster, about twenty metres in length and ten metres in width. It can accommodate hundreds of you in its stomach. You can find a place to sleep in its interiors. Some caves or some holes. You can lay your head among its warm intestines and sleep comfortably there." Sabina, at once, clutched her chin and exhaled noisily. A mixture of anxiety and horror filled her mind.

"There are little cubs in its stomach. They don't like strangers and will scratch at you," she disclosed. "They will tear your skin with their toe-nails. You will need to be tolerant and friendly to them." Sabina's skin was now wet with horror. Her intestines coiled into one knot of fear. She wondered why they had to experience all that painful torture. Was it worth the while? She wondered.

"Also know that the ogre can decide to vomit you into the sea and all of you will drown. It is her decision. It depends on her mood on that day, or how much she dislikes some of you."

"Excuse me," one girl was so scared that she could not hold herself back. "What shall we do if she spits us into the sea?"

"That is none of my business!" Lokolo-kolo dismissed her, and all the girls burst into laughter, but quickly got remorseful again. The girl who asked the question covered her mouth in embarrassment. "If all of you get drowned, it is bad luck. Yes, bad luck! That is all. The village will sacrifice seven bulls and seven goats and count its losses. Nothing will happen. Life will go on as usual. We shall wait until next year to get another batch of girls for the rite. Life will not stop because you are dead. The village will carry on." The girls were heard exhaling noisily. Sabina shut her eyes in dismay.

"How shall we come back home?" one girl expressed in shock.

"Well," Lokolo-kolo's eyes widened, and grew wild. She raised her vein-lined arm and adjusted her red scarf on her head. The little black serpent peeped from her mouth again, then she spoke: "Well, only the brave girls will come back. The cowardly ones will either be crushed or eaten by the ogre and its cubs, or be drowned altogether. They can also be abandoned by the ogre at the sea."

The girls cupped their cheeks in their palms. Sabina's heart beat rapidly. She narrowed her small eyes into slits and, in her mind's eye, saw the expansive monster crawling with might and rage over angry sea waves, carrying the twelve of them in her stomach, as they screamed and called for help. The monster then rolled over the sea waters, bellowing haughtily.

Sabina's train of thought was interrupted by a nudge from one of the girls. "Let's go!" she told Sabina. Sabina was not aware that Lokolo-kolo had long come to the end of her speech. The girls, in a mood of terror, assembled in groups in and outside the hut conversing about the ogre.

At night fall, supper was brought in by the girls' parents. Sabina's mother brought sorghum and pumpkin. When she looked at Sabina's face she realized that her eyes were wet and red.

"Why are your eyes red?" the mother asked. "Have you been crying?"

"No, Ma," Sabina answered and glanced down to the floor. Sabina decided to ask her mother about the night of the ogre. When she was preparing to start her question, her Ma noticed and warned her not to ask anything concerning the ritual.

"Don't ask me questions," she admonished her. "Ask Lokolo-kolo, or simply wait for the night."

After supper, dusk set in. The hour was fast approaching. The ogre was to come at midnight. Sabina found herself utterly disturbed. As the nightfall came closer, her mind went into turmoil. Thoughts ran through her mind uncontrollably. She was gloomy.

Lokolo-kolo stole to her hut. She lay on her bed to rest before the ogre came. As she lay on her bed she was surprised to hear a knock on her door. She did not imagine any of the girls could gather enough courage to come to her house. She rolled down from her bed made of sisal ropes and timber. She lit the tin-lamp that was on the table. She wrapped her withered bones in an old shawl and tiptoed to the window.

Wrapped in a *leso* and looking so tiny, Sabina stood shivering in the darkness. The wooden window suddenly fell open. A ghostly face peeped out. The wild eyes looked like two overripe oranges on the withered face. Sabina thought she could as well be a witch, going by her strange image and the fact that she led a solitary life.

"Who is it?" Lokolo-kolo inquired, peering into the dark.

"It is me *magokoro,*" Sabina answered

"It is you, who?" she asked, straining her eyes to see.

"Sabina," she said, rather timidly.

"Oh! What brings you here when the ogre is about to come? You should be with other girls." she asked astonishingly, and without waiting for a reply, she vanished from the window. Suddenly the bamboo door swung open. "Come straight in!"

The wall of her hut was made of mud, cow-dung and clay. The thatched roof was covered with a mat serving as a ceiling board. Her house was a jumble of assortments. Different sizes of gourds and calabashes lay about on the floor. There were grain baskets crammed together at the corner. At the other corner chicken cuddled together, cackling and pecking one another.

"Have a seat!" Lokolo-kolo offered her a three-legged stool. Sabina sat and gazed on the floor. "So, what brings you here?"

"You know, *magokoro*—" she began, but a lump came into her throat.

"Just tell me, Sabina," Lokolo-kolo urged, and then threw back the part of her shawl that was spilling over her shoulder. She then sat up to listen.

"You know, *magokoro*—," she was stuck again. Tears welled up in her eyes and she bent to conceal them. Lokolo-kolo looked on and her own eyes itched with tears. She stood and went into her bedroom. Sabina sat up and looked about the room. The tin-lamp flickered and sent Sabina's shadow trembling on the clay wall opposite. The quivering shadow looked like a monster, the anticipated ogre, Sabina thought. Outside, the night was silent, except for the faint noise coming from the group of girls in the other hut. The old lady came back after a few minutes, yawning and trembling with cold. She sat next to Sabina on a stool and held her hands.

"Tell me what brings you here?" She was friendly.

"I am of the opinion that —," Sabina began. She trembled and coughed. "*Magokoro,* I don't want to —"

"You don't want what, Sabina?"

"The night of the ogre is —"

"What about the night of the ogre? Speak!" Lokolo-kolo was running out of patience.

"Kindly *magokoro,* let me—," she got stuck again. She sobbed before Lokolo-kolo and shook with bitterness.

"Alright, you can go now," Lokolo-kolo gave up. "Come back later in the night and you will tell me what it is that you want. Be here before the ogre arrives." Lokolo-kolo stood up at once, an indication that she was done with her.

Sabina stood up, too, and left the hut. The moon was peeping out from among the rifts of clouds and made the night less threatening. She wiped her eyes as she walked on. Birds were twittering on trees and the noise of girls assembled in the hut could be heard.

Somewhere half-way, Sabina stopped. She stood in the dark for nearly half an hour, meditating, pondering. She gathered enough courage and decided to turn back. When she reached Lokolo-kolo's hut, she peeped through the window. The tin lamp was still burning and the clay-walls shone brightly. She knocked. Lokolo-kolo, without hesitation, opened the door.

"Oh, you are back!" she exclaimed, clutching her shawl. "How fast! Just come straight in." When she was seated, Lokolo-kolo asked her: "Now, what did you want to tell me? Have you gained enough courage?"

"I am so disturbed since morning," she said, and explored the wall opposite.

"What disturbs you?"

"I want—"

"You want what? Tell me?"

"I want to tell you—," she started, but stopped. "You know *Magokoro,* I don't want the ogre!" She dropped the bomb shell and broke down, bursting into tears.

"What?" Lokolo-kolo squealed with shock. She stood up and swung her hands up to hold her head before it could drop. *"Wololo!* You don't want the ogre?" She moaned, opened her eyes wide and bent down to peer into her. Sabina's body rocked and shivered. "This year again, you don't want the ogre? When will you have it? Look, you are now over-aged! Other girls call you *omong'ina!* an old woman. You are not ashamed of it? Not ashamed at all? Oh my*!"*

"I don't want it at all!" she got the voice to speak. "I don't want to have it in the rest of my life!"

"My! What devil has entered into your little head?" the old lady asked with shock, brought her thin frame down to her stool and peered into Sabina's face. "If your parents could hear all this!" she exclaimed. "If other girls could know what you are saying!" she hissed. "If the village could get wind of all this!" she wondered, shaking her head.

"They know that I don't want the ogre!" she was determined to fight on.

"What? They know it? Your parents know it?" she bared her teeth and widened her eyes. Her nostrils grew bigger and quivered. Her teeth bit her lower lip. After some time, Lokolo-kolo decided to calm down: "Would you please think about your decision, Sabina. Do not rush in making silly resolutions such as this one. You will regret it later. Furthermore, it is unheard of. It is something no one can imagine of. It has never happened in our village. It is a shame! If it happens it would bring a curse on your parents and on the village as a whole. All of us will be cursed. No one will marry you if you won't face the ogre. Furthermore, your parents will be the laughing stock of the village. Think of that, Sabina. Now, go and revise your thinking."

Sabina stood up and walked out of the hut without a word. She walked through the darkness absent-mindedly. She joined the rest of the girls in the other hut.

The Night of the Ogre

Hours flew by. The night was growing old. It was about eleven. It was the night of the ogre. No girl was allowed to go out or involve herself in any activity when the ogre was about to arrive. Tens of women swarmed into the homestead and gathered in and outside the hut. Others found a place to sit under the hut's eaves next to the bamboo window, while many others sprawled on the field outside next to a big ball of fire. Others sat inside the hut and stoked a big ball of fire lit at the corner of the hut. It burnt with fierce rage and lit the entire hut.

Finally it was midnight. The hour had come. It was time for the ogre. This was a ritual all girls who had to be cut had to undergo. Sabina's mother and all other women in the village had experienced it. Great grandmothers and their mothers observed it. No woman in the village ever escaped this custom. In this village, it is what made them women and wives.

Sabina inhaled and let the breath out noisily. They had been waiting the whole day and the whole evening. The important moment in their lives had finally come. The girls trembled with a mixture of fear and anxiety. Some could be seen sobbing, others clutching their chins in their palms, dumb-founded. Others found solace in prayers while a few others hummed songs.

Suddenly, amid the sighs of the girls and the silence of the night, a big booming voice was heard from afar. It was a big sound that rent the silent night, sending the village onto its feet. It was the ogre. The big monster had finally arrived. The women suddenly rose to their feet. It was the end of a long wait. The hour had finally come. The girls were quickly made to lie down on the earthen floor beside

16

the fire at the corner. Their heads touched the uneven floor and their hands and legs spread apart. The women were heard moving in and out of the hut. Whispers, giggles, exclamations and murmurs filled the dark room. Suddenly there was silence, big silence that raised Sabina's hairs. The silence was suddenly broken by a loud cry from the monster. The ghastly sound caused a cold sweat of terror to break out on Sabina's body and her heart felt as if it would break through her ribs. She shook like a leaf in the wind. She thought about the dragon and her heart froze in her ribs. She swallowed hard and wriggled on the earthen floor, trembling.

"The ogre! The ogre! The ogre!" a solo voice rent the night.

"The ogre has come! The ogre has come!" more voices joined in.

"The ogre!" all the women shouted.

Stamping feet of women rushing in and out of the hut to welcome the ogre was heard. Many others were heard rushing into the hut to fetch one thing or another. Voices whispered in the dark with a tone of urgency. Cries of 'sorry' by people jostling, intermingling and bumping into one another were heard.

"The ogre! The ogre!" more shouts came.

"The ogre is here with us!" all joined in unison.

The entire village joined in the hustle and bustle of welcoming the ogre. Ululation! Cheers! Claps! Dance and song, all filled the hut and the dark night outside. Sabina, at one moment, thought she was dreaming. She was lost, confused; she felt like crying.

She was startled by a second round of shouts: "Hold him! Hold him please!" There was an intense commotion, trampling and jostling among the women. A vibrating snarl rent the air, sending Sabina into a tremble. Heavy footsteps came down on the ground outside with a force that shook the hut, like the initial tremors of an earthquake. Sabina wanted to scream, but her mouth became dry, her lips trembled and bit the earthen floor.

"Tie him! Tie the ogre! Get hold of him!" a babel of voices rose.

"He will kick us! Tie him please!" one woman shouted.

"Oh, God!" Sabina whispered to herself, terror-crazed, holding tightly onto the earthen floor below. In her mouth, she tasted the bitter bile of fear. Suddenly the hut fell silent, a silence that haunted Sabina.

"He is now settled!" a soft voice whispered from the corner of the hut. "He can now swallow each of them silently."

"Oh, look at his teeth!" one woman exclaimed in shock.

"Oh, they are very long and sharp," another replied. "They are like the teeth of a saw."

"Look at his mouth!" another voice wondered.

"It is so huge like a street!" a woman spoke in amazement.

"Check its belly, oh my!" another woman was shocked.

"Inside, it is the size of a stadium," a voice complemented.

"Look at the way he wriggles!"

"He is indeed a great dragon!"

"He is now licking his lips, look!" one woman spoke with a mixture of fright and excitement.

"I have never seen such an enormous tongue!"

"It is the size of two mattresses put end to end!" a voice complemented

"He is hungry! Hungry! He wants meat!"

"Now allow him to swallow them," a voice suggested.

"Yes! Let him swallow them now!" they all shouted in unison.

"Stand up!" the first girl was commanded by the women. Sabina could hear the girl reluctantly rising to her feet. "Get in, let him swallow you!" The ogre whined; his whining rose and fell; he screamed and boomed out.

"Don't hold my *leso*!" a shout came. "Be swallowed alone! Don't pull me in with you, *egesagane eke*!"

Sabina heard the girl screaming and tearing the women's clothes. "Don't hold me! Stupid girl!" an angry voice shrieked. Sabina held her breath, then let it out in a frightening terror. "Be swallowed! Be swallowed by the ogre!" the women shouted. The ogre roared loudly. He bellowed with rage. Sabina's temples pounded and perspiration came into the palms of her hands. There was silence. "Good!" a voice expressed satisfaction. "Pick another girl!"

The next girl was a bit hesitant. "Stupid! Come up! Let the ogre swallow you!" the women shouted at her. There was commotion and a struggle as the ogre's roar became louder. The girl seemed to have put up a fight. "Throw her in! Throw her in!" a strong voice came. "Let her be swallowed!" another one added. "Mama-a-a-a!" the girl was heard screaming. Then suddenly there was no more commotion. The ogre went silent, and the women's voices also died. Sabina knew that the girl had been swallowed. She moved her legs with uneasiness.

Now it was the turn of the girl next to Sabina. Sabina heard her being picked. The bellowing and screaming of the ogre rose again. Sabina's throat closed with panic. Her heart increased in tempo and every beat drummed in pain. "Stop biting me!" a woman's voice came clear. "Whether you like it or not, you must be swallowed!" The girl screamed and fought the women. She became a whirlwind of arms and legs and sharp raking teeth and fingernails. The women lost their hold and clutched badly bitten fingers, cursing. "You are stubborn, aren't you?" an angry voice asked. The girl was seized by all the women as the ogre cried for her flesh. She was thrown in pu! "There you go, stubborn fool!" a satisfied voice said. Silence followed, and only a sound of panting women could be heard. The ogre went silent. Sabina's heart skipped a beat.

Finally, it was Sabina's turn. It was her turn to be swallowed by the ogre. She had escaped this ritual in the previous year and the year before the last.

"This is another stubborn lass who came late for the counselling session," Lokolo-kolo was heard talking. "She did not take the meeting seriously," she added amid a deafening roar of the ogre. Sabina closed her eyes and her mind went blank. She let her body be lifted off the earthen floor by numerous bony hands. She was dragged along the semi-dark room.

"Bring her closer to the mouth!" a voice desperately spoke and the ogre bellowed hungrily. Sabina closed her eyes tightly to avoid the terrible sight of that monster. She fumbled and groped with her fingers, so as to feel the piercing teeth of that mysterious animal. Half-dragged and half-standing, Sabina waited to feel the slimy lining of the monster's stomach. She walked with her feet spread apart waiting and expecting to feel the meaty, bloody, and dungy floor of that monster. She didn't feel any of them. She didn't feel the meaty, bloody and dungy floor; neither did she feel the slimy lining of the ogre's stomach.

When she finally opened her eyes, lo! There was no ogre. There was no animal of any kind in sight. She swept her eyes around the semi-lit hut and only saw the gleaming faces of women seated side by side. The girls who had gone before her had been quietly crammed in one corner of the room waiting for others to undergo the same procedure. She was dragged to the corner of the house where there was a young woman who stooped over a pot whose mouth had been wrapped in a goat's skin. The woman held a greased stick, whose one end touched the skin. She rubbed it rapidly, moving her hands up and down, producing the whining sound of the ogre. Sabina took in a deep breath and let it out in a whoosh of relief. The woman stopped and handed over the stick to Sabina. Sabina rubbed it up and down. She, too, was able to produce the whining sound of the ogre.

"Enough!" the woman whispered. Sabina was then taken outside the house where another young woman stood with a long string, whose end was tied to a ruler. Sabina was given the string and showed how to whirl it round and round, the effect making the ruler to produce a whining sound that was thought to belong to the ogre.

"Enough!" the woman nudged her. She was signalled to join the other girls in the hut.

"This is called an ogre ritual," Lokolo-kolo said after the last girl went through the activity. "The night of the ogre ritual is meant to make you brave. We want women who can take challenges in life; women who can fight alongside their men during war. Not women who will dash under their beds when enemies come knocking at the door. You are now stronger than when you came here."

They had been initiated into the secrets of the first ritual that had been hidden from them all the years. Sabina had heard about the night of the ogre ritual, but the detail of it was not disclosed to her. The older girls who had undergone it kept it a secret and did not reveal anything about it to the young ones.

The following day the girls were released to go back to their homes. "You will stay with your parents for three weeks," Lokolo-kolo addressed them in the morning. "At the end of the three weeks, we shall have the day of the ogre. On that day you will be taken out at night to be bitten by the ogre," Lokolo-kolo said and swept her wild eyes over the girls. The girls stole puzzled glances at one another, wondering what will happen during the day of the ogre. "Tonight the ogre only swallowed you. On that Sunday it will bite you. I think you know what that means. The biting is not going to be as easy as the swallowing that you received tonight," she explained. "This one involves the pouring of blood and you know what that means." The girls looked at one another with frightened faces. The ogre in this case, they knew, meant the cutting of their *gento,* organs. Sabina closed her eyes, and almost felt the pain of the knife coming between her legs. She cringed in terror.

'Becoming' a Man

Sabina walked through the wooden gate of their homestead. Her mother and younger sister rose to welcome her back home. The mother, who knew what Sabina felt inside her, quickly started cheering her up.

"Is everything alright, Sabina?" Ma Sabina asked. Sabina didn't utter a word, but bowed before her and gave her hand out, which her mother held in hers.

"But Ma—" the words stuck in Sabina's throat. Tears welled up in her eyeballs.

"What is it, Sabina?" her mother asked, placing her hand on Sabina's shoulder.

"You didn't tell me what the ogre night was all about," Sabina gasped, her face distorted in bitterness.

"What about it?" her mother asked.

"You could have explained to me that it was all a phony," Sabina complained.

"A phony, or no phony, it is a ritual," her mother half-shouted.

"But Ma" Sabina started but her tongue got stuck in her mouth again, and tears streamed down her cheeks with bitterness.

"The night of the ogre gives your heart strength," the mother said with assurance.

"An unnecessarily fear, Ma," Sabina sobbed. "You can die of fright, Ma," she said, kneading her eyeballs. She blew her nose with the hem of her *leso*.

"It is a ritual whose secret you had to discover yourself," she spoke firmly. "So there is no way I could have explained it to you before you underwent it yourself." The mother took her hand again, and this time led her away into the house. "You now understand it, just like all other girls do," she explained as they crossed the threshold of the main hut. "We also had to discover it by ourselves. Sit and drink porridge. Had you eaten anything?"

"No."

"Let me prepare some porridge for you," the mother said and went out into the adjacent kitchen. She later came in to the hut with a gourd of porridge. She poured it into *egesanda*, a calabash, and handed it to Sabina. Sabina drank it meditatively with beads of tears hanging on the lids of her eyes.

"Be strong like other girls and endure the pain of the next ritual," her Ma encouraged her. "The next ritual will be the ogre day. It will be the cutting," she said. "All of us have undergone the same. I recall I was terrified almost to death. So, it is normal. Take heart, my daughter. When the day of the ogre comes, you will leave home at dawn," she disclosed. "You will be taken down to the valley. Strengthen your heart now. You will have to be brave to face the day of the ogre. It is painful, but you will have to endure it. It is what defines us."

Sabina cringed.

After drinking porridge, Sabina went to sleep in her hut. She woke up at dusk and found her mother in the kitchen preparing supper. When it was ready, Sabina, her younger sister and her mother ate it silently. The nightfall set in and the birds on trees nearby quietened.

"You mean our organs will be cut?" Sabina inquired.

"Yes. Only a slice of it," Sabina's mother explained, baring her teeth, and tightening her lips against the teeth to indicate the tiny amount that will be cut. "You won't feel the pain at all."

"No pain, Ma?" Sabina squealed, her mouth gaping.

"A little pain."

"A little pain, Ma? Why the pain in the first place, Ma?"

"It is a cultural practice that has been with our people from time immemorial."

"But does it have meaning? Other people don't circumcise girls, do they?"

"Other people? Like who?"

"Like Nina, my friend at school."

"Yes, Nina is not cut. Her tribe doesn't circumcise girls."

"Why don't we also stop circumcising, Ma?"

"We are a different tribe"

"We can also stop cutting and be like Nina's tribe?"

"No, we can't be like them. You see, our uniqueness lies in the customs and beliefs of our people."

"Why should we observe these customs? They are retrogressive, Ma?"

"These customs, values and practices bind us together as a tribe."

"But, Ma—"

"Sabina!" her mother shouted and stared fiercely at her. "Enough now!"

"But Ma, not all customs can be of benefit, some are archaic and need to be discarded."

"Don't question our culture, saucy girl!" her mother pointed a finger at her.

"But Ma," Sabina started. "What do we benefit observing such painful customs and traditions?" she asked in earnest.

"Stupid girl!" mother barked. "One who leaves her culture is a fool!"

"I think it is the other way round, Ma," Sabina resisted. "It is those who observe customs that don't benefit them who are fools." Her mother stood up. Sabina was silenced by a slap on her cheek.

"Why do you beat me, Ma?" she asked, clutching her burning cheek.

"Don't be stupid! You are asking too much for your age!" She pushed her away. Sabina tottered to the floor and fell on her back with a thud. She sat up quickly, sobbing. Her mother fumed her way into the inner room and came back with a stick. "Stand up, saucy girl!" her mother commanded. Sabina quickly stood up. Her mother looked at her for a while and the anger on her face receded. The stick dropped to the floor. The veins on her forehead disappeared. She then said humbly: "My daughter, you know you are right. This practice has no meaning at all. But your father will kill me if he finds out that I am siding with you on this. He will kill me. He will kill me, my daughter."

"Kill you Ma?" Sabina spoke softly and seemed to empathize with her mother. "Why, Ma? It is a negative practice. It has no meaning. You, too, know that!"

"True, my daughter."

"We were taught at school that it causes health problems," Sabina said as she wiped her tears.

"That is true, my daughter," her mother spoke, empathy in her voice.

"One can develop a lump on her organ, like the one I see on Kwamboka."

"Kwamboka?" the mother curiosly asked.

"Yes, that girl from the other side of the river. I saw it when she came to the river to take a bath. She even openly sat on the stone and bared it to us. A big lump, Ma!" Sabina said and expressed the size of the lump with her hands.

"Oh!" Mother exclaimed.

"Oh, you see, Ma, a harmful cultural practice!" she half-shouted, bitterness in her voice.

"Your father cannot hear any of that," her mother regretted and looked at Sabina with a stern face.

Shortly, the duo heard noise from afar. It was Sabina's drunken father. The old man was singing and shouting. "Be quick!" Sabina's mother spoke with a tone of urgency. "He will find fault with you if he finds you here."

Sabina quickly darted out of the hut and entered her small hut that stood a few metres away from the main one. She bolted the bamboo door and rushed into her bedroom. She threw herself onto her wooden bed. She then listened to the goings-on outside. Her father's song floated clearly into her hut:

> Sabina, my daughter, go in for the cut
> Let the knife mould you into a woman
> For mama and my sake endure the hurt
> And let the village see me as a total man

Sabina held her breath as she listened to word after word, spilling through the air, hitting the eaves of the house, filtering through the cracks of the wall, reaching her with astonishment. When he was nearer the homestead, his song became more intense and clearer.

> With courage, face that terrible ogre
> Don't move from the initiation stone, don't run!
> Endure the pain and be able to conquer
> Only in conquering would you make me a man
> Only in conquering would you make your mama a woman
> Only in conquering would you become a woman

The old man tottered through the gate, staggering along the footpath that led to the main hut. When Sabina gets the cut, he thought, he will be respected as a man in the village. For now his age mates referred to him as *enana,* a child. He was not happy with the term. Neither was he impressed with the conversation that had transpired at the drinking party that evening. One friend referred to him as "the father of a stinking kitten!" While another called him "Pa of the filthy girl." The worst term was coined by another of his friend: "*enana*, a child!" He was a child, so long as he had not circumcised his first-born daughter. This term infuriated him.

"Who is *enana?*" he had asked.

"You, you are *enana*," the friend had replied.

This conversation nearly broke into a fight. Now as the old man tottered along, he recalled the chat and bit his lower lip in bitterness. He had to be a man, urgently, soon, he thought. Sabina was definitely the key to that manhood he badly craved for. When she gets the cut, successfully, there will be drinks and food galore in his homestead for people to celebrate. He will be referred to as a man. His name will be colourfully packaged in songs. After the cut, Sabina will be marked for marriage. On her marriage day, the old man's home will be abuzz with drinks and food. People will eat and drink and call his name in songs. He will be elevated to higher status — a man! — with a married daughter. He will join the rank of other men. He will be eligible to become the clan headman. He will qualify to sit among the council of elders who made decisions in the village. He will simply be a man. His friends will cease making demeaning comments about him at beer parties.

When Sabina's dowry is paid he will use it to marry another wife. Two wives will be better than one. He will join the ranks of men with two wives, a rank superior to the rank of men with one wife. He will be referred to as *omoruoti*, a wise elderly man.

"Sabina," the old man called out aloud. "Where are you, my daughter?" He then banged on the door of the main hut. Ma Sabina quickly opened the bamboo door before her man's patience ran out. The old lady, as always, came face to face with that crumpled figure lying motionless in the doorway, red blank eyes and a drooling mouth. Normally she would support it walk into the hut, bathe it in warm water, give it something to eat and place it on the bed; and finally cover the "corpse" with a blanket. At times it will wet the bed with its vomit and mucus, while grumbling and uttering incomprehensible words: "I married you in the month of June!" the now half-conscious figure would chant, tossing his head on the bed. "Around the hour of noon!" he will exult. "My wife, listen to this tune! While out there shines the moon!" He will then become all bluster and brag. He will say that he used to be a very good singer and a popular dancer when he was a young man. He will then go ahead to explain how he won the hearts of many girls in the village. "You are lucky," he will say, "that I married you when there were many beautiful *titis* in the village who were dying for me."

His wife normally would ignore his chants and songs, till, after a while, the chant and song would be replaced with a munching of lips, a kicking of legs and the throwing up of hands. It would then be another while before his theatrics are replaced with heavy snoring. In the morning he would deny having snored or drunk any beer the previous day. His wife would nod her head in agreement with him.

Three Rats

The rays of the sun pierced through the cracks in the clay wall. Sabina turned over in her bed, rolled down and dressed. She walked out and went to the main house. Her father, who was sober and drinking porridge, told her: "Sabina, I want you to go down to the field and collect firewood after your breakfast. You can also use a sack to carry some of the big dry wood that was split last month."

"Yes, Pa, " she replied.

Sabina emptied her calabash of porridge and picked a *panga* and an axe from her father's house. She also took with her a sisal sack which she gathered into a small ball and strapped round her waist. Walking through the gate along a narrow footpath that ran down to the open field, she went beyond the field and reached the forest by the river. Here, she picked the few pieces of wood she could get and came back from the dark interior. She tied the pieces of wood with a rope and inserted the bundle into the sisal sack. When she was about to lift the bundle onto her back, she heard a voice from the bush nearby.

"Egesagane eke!" the voice came.

She stood straight and looked in the direction where the voice came from. There was no one there. She swept her eyes in all directions, but could not see anybody. When she turned her head to her left, she caught a glimpse of little heads vanishing behind the bush. She fixed her eyes there until the little heads appeared again. There she caught them! Three young girls were hiding behind the bush, sneering and wielding sticks.

"I can see all of you! Little rats!" she blurted out at them.

When they heard "rats" they craned their necks out, stared at Sabina, wielded their sticks and then sneered at her.

"We are not rats!" one of the girls retorted. "You are the one who is a rat!"

"You giant rat!" the second girl added.

"You uncircumcised rat!" the third shouted and, with the palm of her right hand, demonstrated the act of cutting.

Sabina's face grew dark with fury. She left the bundle of wood and walked towards them. "What did you say?" she asked and before they could answer, she threw her full weight over the fence and reached the ear of one of the girls. She grabbed it and squeezed it between her fingers. The girl gave one loud yell that rent the still air of the forest. The other two girls escaped into the woods. Sabina pulled the girl by the ear over the fence as she whined and pleaded for forgiveness.

"Please I will not call you *egesagane* again," the little girl pleaded. "Please forgive me! Forgive me, Sabina!" she begged. "Sabina, my dear friend!"

"Will you do it again, little rat?"

"No, please, forgive me, Sabina," the girl beseeched.

"Am I *egesagane?*" Sabina asked, and dug her fingernails deep into the skin of the ear.

"No, you are not," the little girl moaned, closing her eyes to assuage the pain.

"What am I?" Sabina asked, her teeth biting her lower lip.

"You are cut, you are a lady," the girl sweet-talked her.

"Repeat those words for my ears, please," Sabina commanded

"You are cut, you are a lady."

"And you? What are you?"

"I am *egesagane,*" the girl said, tears coursing down her cheeks. "I am *e-ee-ge-sa-ga-ne.* plea-se for-gi-ve me-e-e-e."

"Say 'I am a rat'," Sabina commanded the little girl.

"I am a rat!" the girl repeated after Sabina, her eyes tightly closed in pain.

"I want you to learn a lesson," Sabina said, squeezing and twisting the ear hard and pulling it towards her over the foliage. The girl cried and screamed out for help. She called the names of her friends and her mother, but none came to her aid. Sabina then let go the ear and pushed her by the temple. The little girl tottered and fell to the tall grass over the other side of the fence. She then quickly stood up, wiped her face and, looking at Sabina, bared her teeth at her.

"Egesagane eke!" she shouted at Sabina. *"Egesagane eke!"* she repeated.

Sabina moved closer to the fence again, and threatened to jump over.

"Egesagane eke!" the girl repeated. Before Sabina could bend and find the weak point in the fence through which to squeeze her body, that rat of a girl skipped and gnawed her way into the woods, following the path on which the other two rats had escaped.

Sabina stood there, staring blankly into the woods, her mouth gaping, reflecting on the incident. *Egesagane!* The uncut! The term was so offensive that it smelt, it stank, it irked. She felt like crying. If she were circumcised, she could fare on well with her age mates and the rest of the village girls. She could be loved by her mama and papa. She could be respected in the village and could be called upon to participate in community functions. She could be a flower girl during wedding ceremonies. She could participate in songs during circumcision ceremonies. To remain uncut continued subjecting her to unpleasant moments, embarrassment and trouble with other girls. She wished she had been cut. She wished she had endured the pain the previous year and done away with it. But, how can she go in for the cut when she already knew of all the health problems that came with it? Won't she be doing something wrong to simply please others? If her mother and father really loved and respected her then they should give her the freedom to choose what to do with her body.

Sabina bent down to lift her bundle of firewood. As she was negotiating with the clumsiness of the load, she heard a rustling sound from the other side of the fence. She raised her slight figure and peered into the woods. Before she could make out what it was, an old lady squeezed her stout body through the loose part of the fence and, in a split second, reached for Sabina's blouse.

"Tell me, why you beat my daughter?" the old lady asked, fuming with anger. The little girl stood behind her mother, exuding power and spewing venom.

"Mummy, she pinched me. Pinch her as well!" the little girl goaded her mother.

"Tell me why you beat my daughter? Why?" The old lady was portly and her arms were huge like those of a boxer. Her eyes were small and piercing. They looked down at Sabina with fierce, burning fire.

"She abused me," Sabina said, trembling. Her mouth became dry.

"How did she abuse you?" the old lady asked, and tightened her grip on Sabina's blouse. She pushed, shoved and almost strangled Sabina by the neck. Sabina swallowed to relieve the strain.

"She called me *egesagane*," Sabina defended herself and moistened her dry lips.

"*Egesagane?* Where is the mark the word left on you?" the lady shouted down at Sabina and poked her cheeks with her fingers. Sabina blinked her eyes.

"It is not there," Sabina murmured, a tremble in her voice.

"It is not there? So, now, who is *egesagane* in this case?" she asked and poked Sabina's cheeks with her fingers. "It is you!"

"Yes, it is me," Sabina accepted.

"You are *egesagane,* a hundred times," the lady emphasized, shaking with anger. Looking up at the lady, Sabina was terrified. Her body shuddered. The old lady raised her hand to the air, and Sabina's intuition brought her hands up to her face to ward off a blow that was coming. "Wo!" Sabina exclaimed. "Wo-o-o-o!" she screamed as the woman rained blow after blow on her head. The slaps sent her reeling down to the grass.

"Please forgive me," Sabina begged. "Oh, please forgive!" More and more blows rained on her head, face, temples and nape.

"I forgive you? Did you forgive my daughter?" the old lady heaved, kicked her stomach and pulled at her hair.

"Mama, she didn't forgive me," the little girl joyfully poured venom. "Why the hell does she think you can forgive her?"

"Please, forgive me," Sabina begged, sobbing, raising her little hands to ward off the blows.

"No forgiveness," the little girl added. "Beat her more Ma, she is not feeling those blows. I want to see her dead, Ma."

"Will you touch my daughter again?" the old lady asked. She bared her teeth at Sabina and raised her fist.

"No please!" Sabina said and looked up at the lady with pleading eyes.

"Don't look at my mother like that!" the little girl threatened." You might bewitch her with those small eyes of a devil!"

"You are *egesagane!*" the stout lady hissed. "You are an uncut, filthy, stinking creature!" She then stood back and looked down at Sabina with red hellish eyes. "You are over the age of circumcision. You are a disgrace to your papa and mama. They can't even share beer with others at parties, or celebrate with others at ceremonies because of you. *Egesagane eke!*"

She then kicked Sabina on the belly. "Do yourself a favour and go in for the cut," she said, calming down. "You hear? You should not miss this year," she added. "You miss this year, you will miss forever. Get the cut and bestow respect to your papa and mama. They are suffering humiliation in this village because of you. Silly girl! Stupid lass! *Egesagane eke!*"

"Uncut rat!" the little girl added. "Shame!" she then sneered at her, placed her hands at her hips and gyrated the hips with contempt.

"Never touch my daughter again!" the woman warned, calmly now, and poked her finger gently on Sabina's cheek. "You hear?"

"Yes," Sabina answered.

"She is daft, she won't hear!" the little girl intruded. "She is as daft as a brush!"

The little girl then thrust her fingers between Sabina's legs and lifted them to her nose. "Smell it!" she said to Sabina. "It stinks! Shame! Get the cut!"

The portly lady grabbed her little daughter's hand and walked away. She pushed through the fence and, once on the other side, disappeared into the woods. Sabina was left wiping her eyes. She touched her face that was swollen. It was covered in blood.

"Mama-a-a-a" she moaned. *"Mama-a,-a-a,* where are you *mama-a-a-a?"* She sobbed, wiping her rumpled skirt and blouse. She lifted the bundle of firewood and placed it on her head. Heaving and coughing, she walked home.

Once she got home, she threw her bundle of firewood on the grass. She placed the palm of her right hand on her face and burst into a scream. Her mother walked out of the hut.

"What is it, Sabina?" Ma Sabina asked shockingly, moving towards her daughter.

"That girl, Bitengo!"

"What did she do to you?"

"She abused me as *egesagane.*"

"And the bruises on your face?"

"Her mother came and beat me," Sabina added and burst into a wail.

"Beat you?" her mother asked in anxiety, as she examined her daughter closely. She touched the swollen temples. "What was she beating you with?"

"Her hands and her finger nails," Sabina stammered, wiped her nose and coughed. Tears flowed down her cheeks. "Mama-a-a-a!" Sabina sobbed, clutching at her wounded arms and cheeks.

"How can she beat you like this, like a cow?" the mother said, bitterness infused in her words. "Come let us go!" She suddenly grabbed Sabina's hand and led her along. "She will show me her womanhood if ever she is a woman!" the mother dared. "She has to prove that she was circumcised with a crude knife!" She half-walked and half-ran, dragging Sabina along. "If truly she is cut, let her face me!" She spit venom and vitriol as they flew through the gate.

They followed the narrow path that led to the playing field. Once at the field, they walked on until they came to a thick fence at the end of the field. They squeezed through it and followed an indistinct footpath on the grass until they came to a wooded area. They could see a river below as they walked through the dark trees. They finally reached a fence where Sabina had been fought. They squeezed through a gap in the fence and found themselves on the other side. They loped over the tall grass and reached a home which was surrounded by trees. Sabina and her mother stood at the fence.

"Who is there!" her mother called, shaking with fury. "Who is there?"

Ma Bitengo came out of the hut, peered over the fence, and when she spotted Sabina and her mother, picked a big stick from the ground and walked threateningly towards them.

"What have you come to do here?" Ma Bitengo shouted angrily. "You infidels!"

"I want you to explain why you beat my daughter!" Ma Sabina roared, shaking with anger.

"And if I don't tell you, what will you do?" Ma Bitengo replied standing at a safe distance behind the fence.

"I will smash that big head of yours!"

"Good! Come over and smash it now!" Ma Bitengo dared. "If you are a woman, do it! Here it is!"

"If you are circumcised, come out of your homestead!" Sabina's Ma also dared. "Move away from your compound."

"You think I was not circumcised?" Ma Bitengo asked and sneered, placed her hands on her hips and swung them contemptuously.

"You are not. If you are, do come and face me here," Ma Sabina dared.

"Ehe! Ehe! I was cut by a crude knife, you hear? I am not like you who was cut by a mere razor blade."

"You are *enkuri!* A crier!" Ma Sabina shouted.

"What? *Enkuri? Me enkuri?* I never screamed during the cut! I never moved an inch, you hear?" Ma Bitengo was stirred; she moved closer to the fence, wielding her big stick. She lifted it up and hurled it at Ma Sabina. It was late for Sabina's mother to dodge it, and it hit her on the head. She yelled loudly and detached her hand from her daughter.

"Wow! My head!" she wailed. She touched the wounded area on her head. Suddenly she furiously pushed her slender body through the gap at the fence and reached Ma Bitengo. She grabbed her blouse by the neck and shook her. "Why did you hit me with a stick?" Ma Sabina asked and bit her lower quivering lip. "You started it; you called me *enkuri,* " Ma Bitengo spoke, choking and swallowing hard, her eyes rolling about with fright.

"But you are *enkuri,* " Ma Sabina spoke firmly, her head oozing blood, which coursed down to her forehead.

"You are also a stinker! A smeller!" Ma Bitengo shouted, as Ma Sabina tightened her grip round Ma Bitengo's neck.

"Me a stinker?" Ma Sabina asked, shaking her opponent vigorously, pushing her about.

"Beat me; don't just hold me!" Ma Bitengo dared.

"You need foolishness ejected out of this big head!" Ma Sabina recommended

"Yes, fight me now!" Ma Bitengo challenged, raising her head in defiance.

"Stupid woman, good-for-nothing!" Ma Sabina rebuked with anger.

"You are the one who is good-for-nothing," Ma Bitengo defiantly said.

"You are a stinker; your daughter is a smeller, too," Ma Sabina replied.

"It is your daughter who is uncut! She and you are stinkers!" Ma Bitengo said furiously in a bid to encounter the abuse from Ma Sabina.

"You say I stink. Do I stink?" Ma Sabina asked, shaking Ma Bitengo, pulling the latter this way and that, then finally pushing her away. Ma Bitengo tottered and fell to the ground. She remained sprawled on the ground, moaning and calling for help.

"Good for nothing!" she moaned in her prostrate position. "Stinking thing! Smelly armpit! Move the smell out of here! Go! Go!"

"Stand up on your feet if you are woman enough!" Ma Sabina dared.

"Remove your armpit from here!" Ma Bitengo said and pinched her nostrils.

Sabina's mother ran short of words. She stopped talking and just looked at the woman as she writhed in pain on the ground. "I can't argue with a fool!" she concluded and spat on the sprawled body. "People won't tell the difference." She then walked through the fence, grabbed her daughter's hand and walked away.

Ma Bitengo rose to her feet at once, moved to the fence and peered over it. "Go! Go! Mother of the uncut!"

Sabina's mother ignored the avalanche of abuses that came over the fence behind her.

"Mama, she also told me I am over the age of circumcision," Sabina said and clung onto her mother's flowing skirt.

"Don't worry. You only missed two years, but that is not harmful. You will do it this year, after all," her mother said as they walked over the tall grass.

"Even if I don't do it, Ma, I will still be a woman."

"What?" her mother barked. "There is no question as to whether you will do it or not."

"What do you mean, Ma?"

"You must get the cut, Sabina!" her mother said firmly. Sabina looked up at her mother. She had never seen her mother get so furious. She trembled. "See the humiliation you bring upon yourself and upon our family!" They hurried across the tall grass. The sun was bright and hot. It made them sweat.

"It is not a humiliation, Ma, understand."

"What is it, if it is not a humiliation?" her mother asked and suddenly came to a stop. She looked at Sabina with barbaric eyes, her lower lip shaking with anger. "What is it, Sabina?" she shouted, fury lining her forehead. She detached her hand from Sabina's, then, in utter fury, grabbed it again and led the way. They reached the fence they had crossed earlier and crossed it at the same point.

"Should we do things simply because others think they are right?" Sabina asked gently.

"What things?" her mother asked, calmly now. "It is a tradition! A custom!"

"But not all traditions are right, or relevant, mama," Sabina spoke softly, her words tinged with wisdom. Her mother glanced down to look at her, amazed at the display of intelligence in her daughter's words. The old lady felt her daughter was right in all that she said and didn't deserve the admonition she received from her. But her papa... her papa.... her papa, what a man! The real enemy to the family! If explained will he understand? No, he won't! It will be a waste of time. It could even turn tragic.

They walked through dark woods and could hear the river churning and gurgling between the rocky banks. They came out of the woods and followed an indistinct path across the vast field. The sun was overhead and their heads burned and sweat trickled down their faces. They crossed a thorny fence that ran over the tall grass and reached a plain field. They entered a narrow path that finally led them towards their gate. Sabina and her mother arrived home, distraught and dismayed. The old man emerged from the hut.

"Where are you coming from?" he inquired, his little eyes dancing in their sockets. "I am seeing anger on your faces."

"There is no anger, Pa Sabina," Ma Sabina quickly responded, assuming a composed face.

"But it is clear there is anger, where are you coming from?"

"Well, a stroll to Ma Bitengo's home."

"To do what? Have you been fighting?" he roared, veins forming on his temples, his sullen mouth tightening on the question.

"Ma Bitengo beat Sabina," she explained, her eyes opening wide with fright.

"So you went to fight, didn't you?" he shouted out, his limbs jerking.

"No, I went there to find out," Ma Sabina said, wringing her fingers like a little girl.

"And the blood stains I can see on your temples?"

"Bush thorns bruised me as we were coming home"

"So what did you find from Ma Bitengo?" he inquired impatiently.

"She truly beat Sabina," she explained, glanced to the ground and squirmed. "She also insulted me," Ma Sabina added. "She said we are a family of stinkers. We are parents of smellers."

"How did this begin, Sabina?" the old man turned to the little girl, moved closer to her, his chest rising and falling in an anticipated fury.

"You told me to go down to the forest and collect firewood, Pa," Sabina began.

"Yes," the old man said, tightening his sullen mouth.

"I did so. After collecting the firewood and ready to come home, I heard '*egesagane eke!*' When I looked up over the nearby fence I didn't see anybody. When I looked the second time I caught the glimpse of Bitengo and two other girls who were hiding behind a bush," Sabina explained. "I left my firewood and moved to the fence. That is when I got hold of Bitengo and beat her. Then her mother came later to also beat me."

"How many times have I warned you not to fight?" her father roared as he moved closer to Sabina. He took Sabina's hand and asked: "I have always told you never to fight, haven't I?"

"Yes, Pa," Sabina said, and tears readily welled up in her eyes.

"Her friends tease her every time she goes out to look for firewood," her mother came to her defence.

"What? Teasing her?"

"They call her *egesagane.*"

"Shame! Shame Sabina!!" he rebuked his daughter. He turned his head to Ma Sabina. "Shame!" Both Sabina and her Ma kept mum. The old man's limbs jerked and his sullen mouth tightened. He rolled his little eyes between the two of them. "You should be circumcised by now!" the old man barked, gathered the little girl's cheeks between his fingers, lifted her little body up and released it mid-air. The girl crumbled to the ground. She then burst into a scream. "Stupid girl! You keep on embarrassing our family with your filthiness," the old man spat in disgust. The mother looked on, empathy written on her face. Sabina sprang up on her feet and, in a split second, disappeared behind the house, yelling and cursing.

"All your age mates are now circumcised and are soon becoming women!" The old man wielded his walking stick as he looked in the direction Sabina disappeared. He whistled in anger, wielded his walking stick again, and finally decided to walk out of the compound.

A Pot-Bellied Visitor

Sabina walked towards the main house with a sense of misgiving. As she entered the hut, she met her father on the threshold. She suddenly stopped and stood like a block of wood, her eyes fixed in a hot sullen stare on her father's face.

"Go back and greet your visitor!" he spoke, his voice dry and dictatorial; Sabina felt a sharp premonition.

"Vi-vi-visitor, Pa?" Sabina stammered. Her mind went blank. She walked out of the house, her brows drawn almost into a single line, the balls of her eyes dark and dancing. Her heart palpitated and her mind was in confusion. Once outside, she looked on her right and saw, next to a granary, a burly old man with a balding head. He was dosing on a bamboo arm chair. She gathered courage and walked boldly towards him. When she reached where he was seated, the man jerked into wakefulness.

"Yes," he spoke, blinking his eyes rapidly. Sabina looked at his bald head. The hair on half of his head was so unkempt that it was hard to tell whether she was looking at a human or a brute. His hair was like a thorn bush and the nails were a dagger length from his fingers. He was a pot-bellied, burly individual with a bushy beard, a wrinkled face and winged eyebrows above his deep-set eyes. His teeth protruded a little and his long massive nose gave him a rather inquisitive expression. On the whole Sabina hated him and wondered why she had been told to greet him. As questions raced up and down her mind, the man looked up at her and mumbled incoherently: "Hmm I am your visitor today, Sabina."

"Visitor?"

"Yes, your visitor," he said, his massive nose quivering, his teeth jutting out of his mouth like a saw.

Sabina was filled with foreboding. She wandered why he had to be her visitor and not her papa's or mama's visitor. A snake of fear ran down her back. She suddenly remembered Maria, her elder sister. She was visited by a stranger at their home one day. Days later she was captured by some unknown men and taken away to live with the visitor at his home. She had never come back since then. Might this be the same arrangement being made between her father and the old man? She was filled with foreboding.

"Thank you, feel welcome," Sabina said and wanted to cry. She turned and left the old man. When she reached in the house she found that her father had left. Only her mother was present, stirring porridge in a *sufuria*. She broke down beside her and screamed.

"Mama!" Sabina wept. "Why all this, Mama? Why, Mama?" Her mother rose at once and took her by the waist. She dragged her to the corner of the house and sat her down where she calmed her.

"Do not cry," her mother said softly, sadly. "Do not bring embarrassment to your father."

"But Ma, why has that old man come to visit?" Sabina asked firmly, urgency in her voice.

"He is harmless," her mother replied in a soothing voice.

"But papa said he is my visitor?"

"Yes, he is," the mother agreed, "but what is wrong with him being your visitor?"

"It means he is going to take me away," Sabina uttered, and a stream of tears coursed down her tender face.

"But you are now a grown up, Sabina," the mother said hesitatingly. "You are no longer a young girl."

"I am a young girl, Ma," Sabina shouted and sobbed uncontrollably.

"But he is not taking you away."

"He is not, Ma?"

"Not now."

"Not now? So he will take me away one day?" Sabina asked and burst into a sob.

"After the day of the ogre," the Mother said, stammering, not sure what to tell her.

"Even after the day of the ogre, I will not accept."

"Keep your mouth shut, Sabina," her mother barked. "Stop sobbing. The day of the ogre is a week away. You will be ready by then."

"No, Ma. What of my schooling?" Sabina asked, tears washing her tender face.

"You will go back to school for a few days, then the man will come for you."

"No, Mama! No! No! No!" Sabina said amid tears and violent screams.

"Look, Sabina," her mother said, cuddling Sabina's arms and torso in an attempt to calm her down, "I was married when I was your age. And see, I have a family. I am a successful woman."

"But that was a long time ago, Ma. Not these days," Sabina shouted and shook her mother's body, as though intending to tear her into pieces.

"Don't worry about marriage, it is not happening today, neither will it happen tomorrow."

"Mama, after the day of the ogre I will go back to school," Sabina said with finality and suddenly stopped crying.

"Listen, your father is coming!" Ma warned. Sabina quickly wiped her face and threw her slight body on the three-legged stool.

No sooner had she sat than her father thrust himself into the room, fuming with anger. "What is it that I am hearing?" he asked, standing arms akimbo, his legs astride. Sabina and her mother kept quiet. He moved near Sabina, trembling with fury. He normally would strike at such a time whatever was before him. Sabina fidgeted with the hem of her loosely-fitting checked skirt. Her face was tense, washed of all colour so that the pale freckles stood out.

"That one outside is your visitor!" he hissed. "Tonight you will get to know what you are supposed to do. We should do this before the day of the ogre which is only a week away. Go to your house and wait."

Sabina stood up and hurried out of the house. She went into her hut and broke down on her bed and sobbed uncontrollably.

Journey in the Night

The moon sailed across the sky. It seemed to go swiftly because of the fleeting clouds that crossed its face, alternately lighting and darkening the dim way. Sabina peered into the sky and could count the number of dinosaurs, dragons and chariots that formed with the shifting of the clouds.

"Mama, where are we going?"

"I told you to be patient, Sabina"

"What time shall we reach there?"

"It is a distance."

The moon hid behind the clouds. Darkness broadened out and spread its shield over the valleys. Sabina clutched tightly onto her mother's skirt as the procession entered a narrow path that was paved with thick foliage on either side. There was something about the deep, silent woods that frightened Sabina. The clump of shrubs grown together in a thick matting of branches that reached to the ground was a frightening sight. They climbed a rocky hill, silently walking on, panting and sweating despite the chill of the forest and the cold wet stones.

"Mama, tell me, where are we going?"

"I told you not to ask me questions," her mother whispered through clenched teeth and nudged her.

"Shall we reach there tonight?" Sabina asked, rather naively.

"Don't ask me," her mother hissed. "We shall be there anytime soon," she said dismissively.

"So whom are we visiting? This old man?" she asked in a low voice.

"No, not him," her mother answered. "Even if it is he, there is no harm, Sabina."

"What shall we do there?"

"Nothing much, Sabina."

"Why do we visit at night?" Sabina inquired. "Why not during the day, Ma?"

Her mother kept quiet. Sabina looked behind her. There was a fairly long procession. Her two aunts, Moraa and Kemuma, walked far behind the line. Her two uncles, Matei and Kerario, both carrying machetes, walked near the front of the procession. Immediately ahead of her and her mother were her three cousins: Bochaberi, Nyaboke and Nyairabu. The three had dropped out of school to get married after their day of the ogre five years earlier. They lived with their husbands and children far beyond the hills, but had visited Sabina's home to participate in this particular event. Leading the way was the pot-bellied, burly individual, carrying a huge club. Everyone walked silently. The silence was appalling. Even the wind high overhead was only a steady monotone, accentuating the stillness rather than breaking it.

They reached the end of a long stretch of rock. As they went downhill, a sudden chattering squirrel brought them to a standstill. Sabina was afraid. "Don't move!" her father warned. Everyone stood still and the noise of that squirrel vanished, disappearing into the woods. Sabina breathed a sigh of relief.

They reached a big rock that stood like a giant monster. The procession stopped there and looked around. They saw a distant river far below in the centre of the big valley to the west; the river caught a spark of flashing light from the peeping tip of the moon and the land changed suddenly, the dark hollows jealously and reluctantly giving up their obscurity. Sabina felt at home.

They reached the river. As they were crossing it they heard noise emanating from the rocky hill before them. It was a deep, throaty, animal laughter. They had barely left the bridge when suddenly the animal sprang forward and stood before them. It was a hyena. The bald-headed, burly individual with a bushy beard swung his club in a sweeping motion and hit it on the head. It disappeared with a squeal. Sabina breathed a sigh of relief once more.

"Mama, are we about to reach our destination?"

"Yes, we are about." She was softer this time.

The procession stopped suddenly. The old man leading the procession then said: "Wait and listen!"

Sabina held her breath. There was a hissing sound in front of them. "There is something making that sound!" the man added. Uncle Matei pushed himself to the front and took out his torch, and flashed at the clump of bushes before them.

"There! A snake!" the bald-headed, burly individual cried. "A snake!" Everyone scampered backwards. "A cobra!" he cried again. Sabina stumbled backwards with fear, and grabbed at someone's hand. And after a while, out of curiosity, she again pushed forward and, to her amazement and horror, saw a long slithering thing writhing round a branch of a tree. She quickly fumbled for her mother, found her and clutched tightly onto her skirt. Uncle Matei picked up a stone and hurled it at the serpent; luckily he hit it on the neck. It raised its head and twisted its body as it slithered away into the bushes. Everyone breathed a sigh of relief.

"Now it is gone!" Matei exulted. "We can now continue with the journey." The procession resumed.

"Mama, suppose we had stepped on it, what would have happened?" Sabina asked, oblivious of where they were.

"It bites anyone who steps on it."

"Oh, Mama!" Sabina exclaimed, clutched her cheeks and almost whistled. "I fear snakes, Mama!"

"They are dangerous," her mother warned. "Even when you play out at night you've got to be careful."

"The nights, Ma?"

"Yes, it is at night when snakes feed. They come out of their holes to look for insects to eat and water to drink."

"They eat insects?"

"Yes, insects and worms."

After a long walk, the bald-headed, burly individual, stopped again. All others reached him and stood in a ragged circle. They had reached the home of the man. "Here we are at last!" he announced, stroking his bushy beard in the dark and scratching his balding head. His protruding teeth could be seen flashing in the moonlight. He pointed to the gate made of rusty, corrugated iron sheets that stood in a bushy hedgerow. "Welcome in," he said and moved ahead to lead the way. He pushed the gate open and the procession followed.

Dance in the Night

The compound was semi-lit with lanterns and tin lamps perched on small wooden tables in various spots in the vast field. There were four huts whose clay walls shone in the moonlight. Each hut had a granary and a toilet adjacent to it. Lows and bleats attracted attention to the animal shed structure on the left of the homestead. A huge quaver tree stood in the middle of the field. Scattered racquets and mango trees waved their thick branches in the gentle wind, sending ghostly shadows in the moon-lit grassy field.

Huge groups of people seemed to be scattered all over the field. Women sat on the tall grass in the centre of the field near what seemed to be the main house. Men formed a small crowd on the right near a brightly-burning lantern. From the gleaming of their teeth and their chattering patterns Sabina could tell that they were excited and anticipating something. Young men congregated on the left side of the field; they were listening to secular music. Some stood shaking their bodies while others pressed their ears next to a small gadget, which probably was a radio. Outside the hut on the far right, a flurry of activities seemed to be taking place among the women. They were seen going in and coming out of the hut, carrying items and conversing in a tone of urgency. Some women left the activities at the hut and came forward to meet Sabina. They addressed her by name and showered her with excessive kindness. Sabina was surprised at this unusual behaviour exhibited by them.

"How come they know my name, Mama?" Sabina asked, with a tone of naivety.

"They just know you," her mother answered starkly.

"Who told them my name?"

"They know you, Sabina," the mother replied, a tone of impatience in her voice.

"Did you tell them my name? Had you come here before, Ma?" Sabina inquired.

"Well, they know the names of people visiting tonight."

"Oh, so someone had sent our names to them?"

"Yes," her mother said, and tapped Sabina's shoulder as a sign of bringing the conversation to an end.

"Who? And for what purpose?"

"Well, Sabina, don't ask me questions," her mother spoke with finality.

The women sang songs while seated and shortly later rose to dance. Sabina was very impressed with their dance. She was filled with joy and felt like she could join in the dance and be happy with them. They formed circles and shook their shoulders together. They worked their arms and gyrated their hips vigorously. Sabina was good at shaking shoulders and could out do most of them.

"Sit on the grass," a voice said near Sabina. She quickly looked up. It was an old woman who seemed to be the organizer of the activities. Her mother whipped her *leso* and spread it on the tall grass. Both sat as they watched the dances. Others who came with them also found places to sit. Sabina realized that there were more people in the compound than she had thought at first. Some others were shielded by the dark clouds in nooks where the moonlight did not reach. Others sat under the eaves of the huts, while many others sat in the banana plantation at the far corner of the homestead. Sabina wondered why all had assembled here tonight.

What baffled Sabina most was that their songs mentioned her name. Her name was infused in every stanza of their songs. They glorified and cheered her in the songs. Her deeds, appearance, hobbies were all mentioned. The song said that they had been looking for her for a long time, but that at last they had found her. Then they also commented that her future was successful for choosing them as her people. Sabina was filled with a mixture of joy and astonishment. She was unable to know how to react.

Sabina, we have been looking for you
But here you are at last, our daughter
Sabina, we have been waiting for you
But today you have come, our daughter

Sabina was tongue-tied. She nudged her mother for an explanation, but her mother dismissed her, and looked down at her with a stern face.

A woman came along with a kettle, followed by another with cups in a twig tray. They went round pouring hot tea into cups and giving them to the visitors. They handed a cup to Sabina and another to her mother and poured tea into them.

"Drink, Sabina," the woman urged her, using a voice that was heavily laden with kindness and love. When the women had gone away looking for other visitors to serve, Sabina's mother turned towards her and said: "Be prepared, you are the next on the dance arena." Sabina turned round with shock.

"What do you mean, Mama?" she uttered.

"You will be called upon to dance."

"To dance, Mama?" She was shocked. Her fingers trembled a little, and the quiver made her cup tilt sideways and tea spilled onto the grass. "How can I dance here among strangers?" Her mother did not respond but concentrated on the dance that was going on. Sabina, however, felt happy and excited, though apprehensive, at the prospect of having to dance among unfamiliar people. She was all pins and needles waiting to show her dexterity on the dance field. She would shake her shoulders vigorously and she was sure to stun the people. She was ready to show her prowess at shaking her shoulders and gyrating her hips. Her heart, though, beat in her like a roll of drums. Her skin twitched and her knees knocked each other with fright. She imagined how she would blend the shaking of her shoulders with the movement of her feet, then synchronize them with the nodding of her head and the gyrating of her hips—she was overwhelmed with anxiety. Her mother noticed the restlessness in her and turned to ask: "Are you afraid, Sabina?"

"Not really, Mama," Sabina spoke, and reclined her little egg-shaped head on her bosom. Suddenly the women stopped their dance and each went to sit on the tall grass. At the far end of the compound, outside the fourth hut where a flurry of activities was going on, Sabina saw an increased movement of people, jostling and shoving. A little bustle seemed to have started there. Sabina noticed that people had gathered around a certain man. The others, who were around him, seemed to move up and down with urgency. Next, Sabina saw people dressing the man in a dark coat, a neck-tie and inserting a wreath of flowers round his neck. He was being encouraged, patted on the shoulders, and cheered. Young men curved their lips and whistled, while young women ululated. He was then carried shoulder-high and driven along. They placed him in the vast field. The man, carrying a small club, shot forward and walked majestically to the middle of the field. Sabina peered keenly to see who it was. Oh! Unbelievable! Shocking! It was that bald-headed, pot-bellied man who was her visitor earlier. His beard hung down from his chin. His forehead was long and extended to join his bald-head. His hair was a bunch of sisal. His fingernails gleamed in the moonlight. His teeth penetrated outside his beard like a hyena. People clapped their hands and cheered him.

"Go! Sabina Go! Go!" her mother suddenly shouted, nudging her.

"Sabina! Sabina! Sabina go!" people yelled from all sections of the crowd

"Sabina, our daughter! Sabina, our girl!" people shouted in unison.

"Sabina! Sabina! Sabina!" more and more voices joined in.

"Go Sabina! Go!" her mother nudged her, urgently, impatiently.

Sabina thought she was dreaming. She darted her eyes in all directions like a little kitten that had been cornered after pilfering milk from a pot. Her heart beat rapidly; she became nervous and confused. She had attended such dances before, but this time round her feet were restrained by powers beyond her means. She was incapable of coming to her feet.

"Go! Sabina, go!" her mother spoke again. "Do not fear. This is your night!"

"Sabina, our daughter!" people shouted.

"Sabina our girl!" more people added their voices.

Sabina scrambled to her feet, her legs wobbling, knees knocking, and her hands moving clumsily. Fright and fear engulfed her. She looked up to the moon and she felt it was nauseating and vexing. The old man was already jumping up, fighting the air with his club and dancing by himself. He raised his hands to beckon Sabina to join him. Sabina flexed her hands and legs and moved forward. Men cheered and young women clapped their hands. Young men yelled, while young women ululated. The drummer beat his drum vigorously and the women sang with more enthusiasm, as Sabina moved closer to the man. Close by, Sabina could see the long beard that hung from his chin like a goatee. She could see the balding head shining in the moonlight. His unkempt hair on his head looked like a thorny bush and the claws on his fingers made him resemble a hyena. His nose trembled and gave him the usual devilish impression. Sabina felt terrified.

While Sabina pondered, the man moved rapidly at once and grabbed her hand, swung it round and pulled her along in a circle. The drummer beat harder on his drum. People cheered loudly and the women ululated with vigour. Quick and graceful, Sabina waltzed like a queen to the noise of people and the beats of the drum. She took her steps carefully, lifting and landing her feet on the tall grass with grace. She gently curled her small torso and swung round the man with tenderness and grandeur.

"Sabina our daughter! Sabina our girl!" The babel of voices was deafening. "Sabina, our queen! Sabina, our girl!"

When the man detached his hand from hers, people clapped and cheered for the last time. Sabina ran back to her place beside her mother on the tall grass. Her heart was beating fast and her body was covered in sweat.

"Congratulations!" her mother said and patted her on the shoulders.

Sabina was overwhelmed with joy and excitement. She had made it. She had never felt as great as she felt that night. The last time she danced and attracted such immense praise was when she was in standard four. It was the end of the term and the head teacher of her school invited any one to volunteer and dance to the beats of the drum. The drum was played by a standard four boy. Sabina volunteered and, without an iota of fear, danced her heart out. The entire school went wild about her fearless nature and feat of performance. Tonight as she sat beside her mother, she felt ten times overwhelmed. In her mind she saw the picture of the old man and her soft steps and, in whole, concluded that she didn't hate him after all. He was nice and made her cheerful. He had danced so well and attracted applause from all sections of the crowd.

"Mama, did I dance well?" Sabina asked breathlessly.

"Yes, very well, Sabina!" the mother said enthusiastically. "You have made everyone happy. No one has so far danced so well as you tonight."

As Sabina was talking to her mother, a group of women came along. They bowed before Sabina and held her hand. Her mother urged her to stand up and go with them. The women, holding her hand, walked along the huts. They passed by the first hut and Sabina peered into it. It was well clayed and a tin-lamp burned inside, revealing shadows of children who sat forlornly on the bare earthen floor. Maybe they had taken their supper and were not satisfied, Sabina thought.

They went past the second hut and the third amid claps and cheers from people. When they reached the fourth and last hut, the women stopped at the door. More women then joined them. The group of women in the field started to vanish.

"Now, kneel," one woman requested Sabina. Her mother pressed her head gently down to the ground. Sabina fell on her knees. One woman came out of the hut and brought blood in a cup. A goat had been slaughtered from which they got the blood. Her mother helped her sip from the cup. She was then led into the hut. The hut had a bed that stood in the corner near a window. The bed was decorated with flowers, beads and wreaths. The walls were smeared with white clay and cow dung. The roof seemed to have been newly-built with a fresh thatch. The wooden window and door both looked new.

"This is your house, Sabina," one of the women intoned as they were sitting on arm chairs placed near a table. Sabina was shocked and she looked at her mother, who ignored her gaze. "After the day of the ogre you will come to live here."

"Be brave during the day of the ogre," another woman encouraged her. "Your success during the day of the ogre will determine whether you will occupy this house or not."

"We wish you success during the day of the ogre!" the third woman said and shook Sabina's hand.

Sabina's heart sank. She looked up to her mother, who intentionally avoided her glance. A group of people came in: three old women and the bald-headed burly individual who had danced with her. The three women were carrying containers. They sat on the empty arm chairs at the corner of the hut. Then shortly they stood up and came forward. They held Sabina's hand and placed it in the old man's hand. They opened the containers they were carrying and poured their contents into one cup. It was milk, which they poured into a cup and gave both of them to sip from. After this short, simple ritual, the women left the hut one by one. Sabina was left with her mama. "Ma, when are we going back to our home?" Sabina asked, confused, bewildered.

"We shall go, don't worry," her mother replied.

"When?" Sabina asked, looking straight into her mother's face.

"We shall go soon!" her mother said, and nudged her with her elbow. The old man sat silently on his arm chair and was not conversing with anybody. Outside, the noise and conversation of people had subsided mysteriously. Shortly Sabina's mother went out. Sabina was left with the bald-headed, pot-bellied man. She peered at the floor.

"Welcome, Sabina," the old man started. "This is your house. After the day of the ogre you will come to live here." Sabina was shaking with terror. She looked out and the night was one sheet of darkness. The lanterns and tin lamps seemed to have been taken away. The light from the moon was no longer there. Tears welled up in her eyeballs and rolled down her cheeks. "Come over and sleep, now," the bald-headed, burly man said, scratching his massive nose. The grey beard seemed to have grown longer and scary at the passing of each second.

Sabina took in a deep breath and let it out in a whoosh of terror. When Sabina hesitated, the burly man stood up and moved towards her. Standing next to her, he stroked his bushy beard and scratched his massive nose. His wrinkled long forehead, winged eyebrows, and the massive nose, blended to give him rather a ghostly impression. Suddenly he held Sabina's hand. She was frightened. He pulled her up and dragged her along. Sabina's thoughts raced fast within her mind. She jerked her hand out of his, turned round and, at once, flew towards the door, pushed it open and flung out of the hut. But the pot-bellied man was fast. He caught up with her outside the hut and grabbed her tiny wrist in his massive hands. He brought her back.

"Do not bring embarrassment, Sabina," he begged. "Don't spoil the ceremony."

"Stop! Don't pull me like that!" Sabina grumbled, trying to disentangle herself from the clammy old fingers. "Leave me alone!"

"Look, don't bring embarrassment here!" he spoke with command, but also pleading with her.

"What do you want to do with me?" she asked, a tone of rebellion in her voice.

"Nothing, just come in," the old man urged, and managed to drag her back to the hut. He left her standing while he walked back to lock the door. Sabina's heart beat rapidly. Having closed the door, the man went straight to spread the bed, and then came back to her. He urged her to go and sleep on it. Sabina hesitated and looked around nervously. When the man's eyes were not on her, she jumped onto the bed and pushed the creaking window open. She fell headlong onto the stones outside below. The man adjusted his bush of beard, pinched his massive nose, protruded his set of teeth out of his mouth and, carrying his pot-sized belly onto the bed, dived out through the window, too. He fell prostrate upon the little girl's body. Sabina gave a little scream under his massive weight, but quickly and cleverly squeezed her small body out of the massive hands and slipped away. He also rose quickly and reached for her legs and Sabina almost faltered but with a little effort she managed to pull her heels from his frail old fingers. Sabina then summoned all her energy as she thrust forth into the dark night. She ran across the vast field, panting and sobbing. She glanced back through the darkness and could not see a figure. She flew through the darkness, puffing and gasping. With her eyes closed, she propelled her hands forward and backward, burrowing through the night. She had reached somewhere in the middle of the field when she suddenly bumped into a wall of flesh. She tottered to the ground. She looked up, heaving and palpitating. A hand cuddled her and held her up.

"Sabina!" a voice called. "It is your mother, Sabina!" the woman whispered, and Sabina looked up and gave a long wail of relief. "Don't run away my daughter!" Terror was in her mama's voice.

"Mama!" she whispered, out of breath, terror-crazed, hysterical, tears rolling down her face. "Are you the one, Ma? Tell me, Mama!"

"Yes, I am the one, Sabina," she whispered. She then cuddled Sabina's tiny body and encircled her hands round her small frame. "Don't sob, my daughter, I am here for you!"

"Mama, are you the one?" Sabina asked again, looking up, breathing heavily and holding onto her.

"Yes, my daughter, I am your mother," she said for the umpteenth time, and bent down to peer at her face. Sabina saw her mother's face in the dark, and thought she had grown old; she looked ghostly and worn out in the darkness. She peered at the face for a long time, breathless, like someone locked up in a dream.

"Why all this, mama?" she finally asked, gasping, releasing her breath in a whoosh of relief. She leaned her small body upon her mother's bosom.

"Don't worry about her for now," a voice came from within. "Don't worry about her."

It was another woman. She had been there but Sabina had not noticed her presence. Shortly, three men came along. Sabina was able to notice that one of them was her father and the other was uncle Matei. She didn't mind them, not now. Her father was calm and silent. He whispered to Sabina: "Go and sleep with your Mama." Sabina's hand was led by her mother and the woman and taken to the first hut on the left. Her heart beat gently in her ribs and had grown calmer. As Sabina entered the hut silence was loud. Women sat on stools and on long benches, with their chins cupped in their palms. They looked upset, tormented and troubled. Sabina heard someone saying: "Do not worry about her for now. She can make it up after the day of the ogre. Nothing is lost."

"The day of the ogre is only a week away," another voice added.

"She has broken no taboo!" another voice whispered from the corner.

Sabina breathed a sigh of relief. After some time the women were snoring and breathing heavily. Sabina was unable to fall asleep.

Journey Back Home

When dawn came Sabina felt relieved. Her mother, father, aunts, uncles and relatives were up and ready to start the journey back home. Soon the procession back home was underway. Sabina's aunts and uncles led the way out of the homestead. Sabina and her parents followed. Behind them were the bald-headed burly individual and his entourage who were driving about fifty cows along. Sabina wondered where they were taking the animals. Sabina stole a glance at the burly man from time to time. His bushy beard had been thoroughly brushed. His wrinkled face had been oiled and looked relaxed. The sisal on his head had been combed backwards and looked like a neatly-placed greased hat. The excess size of his belly had been reduced by the oversized coat he wore. On the whole he was smart and spruced. Sabina lost interest in him and clutched at her mother's skirt.

"Mama, what are the cows for?"

"They are bringing them to our home."

"What for, Mama?"

"The cows are for your father."

"Why should they give them to Pa?"

"Sabina, you will understand all these," her mother dismissed her.

Sabina was filled with misgiving. She recalled the time before her elder sister was captured and taken away. The man who married her had driven in many heads of cattle. Sabina feared for her life. She thought of school and her friends. She thought of high school and university and suddenly tears welled up in her eyes. She pressed her eyes to stop her tears.

"Why are you so sad, Sabina?" her mother asked. "Wipe your

tears, and stop behaving like a small child," she said angrily. "You are no longer a small child."

"Mama, I am bewildered," Sabina said in a moaning voice.

"Don't behave like *egesagane;* you are now a grown up woman."

"I am too young, Mama," Sabina replied, and tightened her grip on her mother's skirt.

"After the day of the ogre, you will be a woman," her mother said, looking down at her.

"But I am not."

"You will be!" she shouted.

The procession went across the vast field almost quietly. They walked downhill towards a valley filled with dense woods. They moved under a thick canopy of tall thick trees. Chirps from the birds spilled in from the nests above. Sabina listened to the sweet sounds and was very pleased. Birds! she thought, have freedom. "I wish we girls had the same freedom as the birds!" she said to herself. "Freedom to fly about, to do what we think is good for us."

The sun's head peeped behind a hill ahead. Its rays pierced through boughs, twigs and perforated foliage of the canopy. Sabina watched the glamour of the sun's rays as they filtered through the woods, reaching the ground in trembling circles. Sabina looked back and admired the long train of animals, as they trod in single file through the dank woods.

When they were out of the thick woods they saw a river below. As they approached the bridge, Uncle Matei gave a cry. The procession suddenly stopped. "Snake!" he cried, then went silent. People released their breath. "Oh, no, it is dead!" he announced." It is the one we killed last night!" Sabina was curious and wanted to see its size; she hurried past several people in the procession and reached the spot where it lay, covered and surrounded by a trail of ants which were winding in a steady black stream over its flesh.

Someone picked up a stick and pushed the carcass out of the way and the procession continued their journey. They were now crossing the river. The water swirled and heaved on the rocks, spewing bile-green weeds along the shore, defying anyone to try his or her skill of crossing it on foot. Sabina stood on the bridge and gave way to others in the procession to go by. She threw small stones into the waters and watched them get swallowed by the waves. She picked up small sticks and hurled them down and watched with joy as they danced on the waves. When the last person, but the cows' owners, passed by, Sabina sprang forward and hurried past the people and reached her mother, grabbed her hand and walked beside her.

The day was now clearing and Sabina could see who was in the procession. The women's heads were covered in *shukas* while the men clad themselves in thick coats. Every man seemed to have carried a weapon. Her father had a spear with him. Her uncles were carrying huge clubs each while other men carried arrows and bows.

They climbed over a rocky hill covered in thick woods. The canopy above was so thick that the sun could not reach them. The dark tunnel of trees and thick canopy was filled with the sound of the rushing wings of birds. Sabina heard the wild cry of a black bird and the hoot of an owl in the nearby tree and looked up, but could not see any of them.

They were finally out in the vast field. The thick canopy in the rocky hill was behind them. Sabina looked down at the canopy and thought it made a big blanket that covered the entire valley. From where Sabina stood, she could hear the churning and swirling of the river below.

The sun had now become intense and Sabina started to sweat. She wiped her pullover and felt a cold breeze come over her. They were now walking on a field that was filled with chrysanthemums and scattered bushes. Sabina was familiar with this place. This was close to the clearing where she had come to collect firewood and was beaten by Ma Bitengo.

Sabina's father finally stopped. They had reached home.

Back at Home

The procession stood outside the gate for a long time waiting to be ushered in. The animals congregated in the nearby field and busied themselves with grass and hanging foliage of trees, oblivious of the change of environment. A flurry of activities was going on in the homestead in preparation for their heroic entry. Finally a middle-aged man came panting through the gate and by gesture of his hand, the procession were let in. Sabina was allowed to go in first, followed by her mother and father. Her uncles and aunts followed while the rest of the relatives came last.

When she raised her eyes she was shocked to meet glamour and colour in what was once a common place compound. Young girls, clad in red, green, blue and yellow beads, long swinging necklaces and wrist bangles and covered in sisal skirts, banana blouses and rose-flower head gear danced towards them in a pattern. She knew most of these girls. The drummer beside them beat the drum and displayed unique dexterity in modulation and movement. The girls danced round Sabina and the old man's party. Then after the girls, there emerged another group of entertainers: the old women. They were also adorned in red, blue, green and yellow beads, necklaces and wrist bangles. They shook their bodies, cheered, and ululated towards and around Sabina. Sabina looked up and realized that there were other girls outside the homestead who peered over the fence. These were the girls who were young and had not undergone the ogre ritual and therefore could not be allowed to get knowledge of the rituals until their day came.

The women who had danced left the arena and were ushered away to the corner of the field. Then a thin tall, wild-eyed old woman came along. She was covered in a red scarf and carried a long rope. Young men took the rope from her and stretched it out between Sabina's people and the burly man's entourage. She then came straight to Sabina and moved Sabina to the middle of the rope. She had foaming lips and rolling eyes and Sabina thought she was familiar. She peered into her eyes and suddenly realized who she was—Lokolo-kolo!

The two sides started pulling the rope, each to their own side. It was a contest and, acting as an umpire, Sabina's eyes darted from one side to the other. The bald-headed, burly individual and his people pulled hard on the other side and when it seemed they were about to take away the rope, Sabina's people put more effort and moved the feet of their opponents. People cheered and clapped their hands. Sabina looked this way and the other way, drowned by the ululations and noise of the drumming and yelling of people. The men on either side were sweating; their blood veins on their temples swelled and became huge like small snakes. After a long struggle, the rope was seen moving towards the bald-headed man's side and shortly Sabina's people fell headlong towards their opponents' side. This was greeted by the sound of "*Oiye-e--e-e-e!*" from all the people. Lokolo-kolo quickly ran to Sabina and grabbed her hand and walked with her to the winning party, to symbolize that they had won the trophy—Sabina!

This was a mock contest in which the visiting party who belonged to the bald-headed man was meant to win as an indication that they had worked hard to get the woman they so much desired. The winning party assembled themselves and danced along the vast field, while the drummer followed them and beat his drum vigorously. The party carried Sabina shoulder high. She perched on the shoulders of two strong men, while she waved her hand to the people who cheered and waved back at her. She was delighted. She waved at the girls in the homestead and those outside the fence.

Whatever it was, or was to be, Sabina wholesomely felt happy. She had never been so overwhelmed with joy. By the time the young men brought her down from their shoulders, Sabina was sweating with excitement. Her face radiated enthusiasm and joy.

The animals had been driven in and seemed to fill the entire homestead. Neighbours, relatives and friends tethered them at the corner of the compound. Some young men had cut napier grass and were already feeding the animals. Other young people busied themselves with the counting of the herd, while others were changing their ropes, replacing the worn-out sisal ropes with new manila type.

The bald-headed man and his people were seated in one of the sheds constructed by the young men. Five big pots of beer were carried by strong men and placed in the centre of the visiting party. The young men who had helped tether the animals and those who gave napier grass to them and many others from the village were allowed to join the visiting party to drink the beer together.

That afternoon a bull was slaughtered and several hens lost their lives. The visiting party was served with the most delicious of foods. They sang and chanted, conversed and gossiped and laughed deliriously as they ate and drank. In the evening the pot-bellied old man's party bade good bye and left for their homes.

The Day of the Ogre

It was one o'clock in the morning. Sabina heard the sound of a horn, followed by a rapid beating of a drum. Sabina knew the time had come. The time to face the ogre had come. She had to face the ogre in order to become a woman. It was time for her to win her spurs, to prove that she was not a cowardly girl. She leaped out of her bamboo bed and walked through the dark to the corner of the room. She squatted and cuddled her little body in remorse. Suddenly all hell broke loose. Noise! Noise! Noise rent the night. Heavy beats of a drum filled the air. The sound of the horn tore the sky above. Ululations! Cheers! Shouts of mockery! The combination grew louder and huge and became a bombshell that quaked the floor beneath Sabina's feet, shook her tiny body and swayed the walls of her hut. Her small frame of body rocked and shuddered.

"Open!" a voice shouted right outside her hut.

"Open! Open!" more voices joined in.

Sabina's mind was in a tumult. Her limbs trembled. She was filled with terror and horror.

"Open, naughty girl!" a voice added.

"If you hesitate, we shall show you a tailless ogre!" a voice threatened, and this was followed by laughter and mockery.

Sabina stood up and stealthily walked to the wooden window. She peeped through the cracks on the badly-fixed wood and saw, to her amazement and fear, a crowd of women clad in head scarves and *lesos*. Among them were little girls clad in scanty tattered *lesos*. They were shivering in the cold night. Their teeth were chattering and their jaws danced in the windy night.

"Open!" a desperate voice came again, amid murmurs, giggles and jeers.

"Since you have refused to open, we shall come in with this bamboo thing you call a door!"

"You over-aged woman, open!"

"You dirty, filthy thing, open!"

"Egesagane eke open!" one threw in abusive terminology

When the door was not opened, the women became furious. They giggled loudly, rumbling at the height of rudeness exhibited by the girl. They unanimously agreed to break the bamboo door and put some sense into the head of that overaged girl. As the enraged ones were about to throw their weight on the bamboo, one woman shouted: "Oh, no-o-o, wait!" They immediately stopped. "We need to talk to her in a friendly manner before we resort to such barbaric action."

"Sure, you are right!" another woman concurred with her.

"Sabina, kindly open," one voice floated through the darkness.

"Kindly open for us, Sabina," another one added.

"You are wasting time for the ogre, Sabina," another pleaded.

The door was not open. Time for the ogre was running out. The other little girls were shivering in the cold wind. Clad in tattered *lesos,* with parts of their bodies exposed to the cold wind, the girls' bodies shook. Their chattering teeth rocked and ground against one another. At long last the women decided to break the bamboo door and get out the rude girl. She would then be kicked, slapped and pinched. She will be made to see the tailless ogre as the women threateningly promised. Being overaged was another of her woes. She will be made to explain why she didn't face the ogre with her age mates the previous year and the year before it.

One woman shouted, "rea-a-a-adyyy!" and all responded in unison: "Go-o-o-o-o!" They threw their weight on the bamboo door and, in a split second, the door gave a squeal sound, then a creaking, finally detached itself from the timber on the clay wall, and it fell into the hollowness of the dark hut with a thud. Some of the octogenarian women landed on the floor with it, their legs shooting into the air, baring their withered thighs and knees, and adding humour and laughter into that dawn drama.

"Flash your torch!" one woman shouted with enthusiasm, as they searched the hut like wild dogs after a rabbit. The women flashed into all the corners, but did not see Sabina.

"Flash under the bed!" another voice advised.

"She is not there!" one woman said.

"Check up in the roof!" a voice came from outside.

The women flashed above their heads, but did not see the girl. The women checked everywhere, and double checked and treble checked, but Sabina was not in the hut. One woman remembered to scrutinize the wooden window.

"Oh!" she cried. "The window is open! She has escaped! She has escaped!" the woman screamed and clutched her cheeks in remorse. The women stood in the darkness, blank-minded, tongue-tied, confused, and unable to know what to do. They went out of the hut and joined others.

The act of escaping was unheard of, abominable and a curse to the entire community. It was unacceptable. It could attract a sacrifice of several goats and cows to cleanse the act by the girl. Before they could conclude on the matter, the women agreed to divide themselves into two groups. The first group was to drive the other little girls down to the river and keep them waiting; while the second group would seek support of young men in the village to help look for and seize Sabina. Men were woken up and were requested to give a hand.

The first group started driving the little girls to the river. The second party immediately started looking for Sabina. With the support from the young men they searched among the dark woods that were around her hut.

"She has not gone far," one woman thought. "She must be within, just within."

"Yes, she will fear the animals in the dark night," another one concurred.

"Let us follow foot-steps carefully," someone advised.

The women scattered themselves and searched silently in the dawn light. No one spoke, but kept their mouths mum. The women, who followed the footpath towards the river, were heard talking loudly. The rest, thinking they had come across the girl, ran in.

"It is one of her sandals!" one woman apologized in a whisper. "It means she is around this point," she suggested.

The women stealthily crept under the hedgerows and thick woods nearby. They flashed their torches into every bush in the fields. After a half an hour, one woman shouted with enthusiasm from the bushes: "Catch her! Here she is! Run here women!" Other women ran in, but it was too late. Sabina crept under a thick hedgerow which the old women could not penetrate and escaped their clumsy, vein-lined, feeble hands. The women now searched more vigorously, following the beaten bush on which she ran.

Sabina crept under thick undergrowth in the middle of a bush. She stashed her head under it, leaving out her legs. Her heart beat rapidly. She could hear murmurs and whispers around her, but she didn't move. But after a while, fear engulfed her. A sense of insecurity overweighed her mind. She crept out of the undergrowth and crawled on her belly towards a denser bush nearby. She squeezed and placed her small body comfortably among the foliage. Suddenly she heard a step nearby, and one flash of a torch. She held her breath and closed her eyes. The trees and foliage around her matted into a thick wall which could not be penetrated by the light from the women's torches. Her body shivered though and she realized she was wet and frozen. She heard the patter of feet at the nearby footpath, accompanied by a bustling sound. She was shivering with terror. I will be caught, she thought. She quickly crawled on her belly towards the river. She could hear the water flowing down the valley. She squeezed her small body through the bushes and managed to reach the river bank. She dropped down into the water.

"Oh, my!" she cried. She almost drowned. She held onto huge roots of trees on the bank and reached for the big tree beside the water. She held onto the rocks and reached a cave. She stashed her small body in it. Huge stones created a roof and a concrete wall around her. Before her eyes was a fierce river. Its waves meandered roughly down the valley of trees and rocks. Her heart beat in her like a roll of drums. Her eyes darted in all directions. The moon suddenly peeped from the rafts of clouds and brought the river to life. Sabina watched as the water meandered down its banks of trees and rocks, and for a while forgot that she was a fugitive.

The cave was warm. Despite the cold wind, Sabina started dosing. Her heart quietened. Suddenly a sharp light was flashed before Sabina's eyes. She startled up from her sleep, and fell backwards with fear. Tongue-tied and bewildered, her mouth became dry and she could not scream.

"Here she is!" a voice next to her shouted.

Sabina had been caught. Clammy fingers, vein-lined hands and boney palms grabbed her torso, limbs and head so tightly that she could not attempt an escape.

"Forgive me, please!" Sabina pleaded.

"Saucy girl! Wasting our time!" a soft but angry voice came.

"You will explain why you are doing all this!"

"Stupid girl! Big for nothing!"

"Filthy thing! Dirty thing!"

Sabina was half pushed and half dragged along. She was walked over tall wet grass, along rocky footpaths and squeezed through thick hedgerows. Her forehead, temples and cheeks were bruised, her eyes streamed with tears, and her bare arms were covered in blood. They finally joined the other group of women and the little girls by the river bank.

"Here is the naughty girl!" the women shouted as they dragged her along.

"Where is that stupid thing?" the women by the river bank shouted.

"Bring her here so that we show her what it means to become a woman!" they added.

"We shall show her a tailless ogre!" one woman threatened. She slapped her across the face. Another one kicked her on the thighs and others pinched her cheeks.

"You think you are cleverer than all of us?" one woman mocked her and pinched her nape.

After the pinching, slapping and kicking by the woman, Sabina was thrown into the shallow waters. She joined others who were splashing themselves with cold water. Someone followed Sabina into the river and immersed her head below the water, left it there for a while, then lifted it up to the surface. Sabina was left shaking her head like someone who had been stung by bees. She breathed heavily and gurgled, swallowing in quick succession. She opened her mouth widely, and burst out into a scream.

"Stop crying, naughty girl!" one woman shouted, and climbed down to the river. She dipped Sabina's head into the water again, left it there for a while, lifted it out and dipped it again. "The ogre eats you well when you are cold!" she explained her action. Sabina sobbed, and breathed heavily, swallowing, gurgling and wiping the water from her nostrils and eyes.

"The ogre will enjoy your meat when it is frozen," another one shouted from the bank of the river.

When the girls' bodies were numb enough, they were driven in a single file up the hill. The trees towered above their heads as they followed a narrow path. The rocks were huge and knocked their bare feet until they bled. Some of the little ones were tired and breathed heavily. It was against custom to support any of them. Difficulties and challenges were part and parcel of the ritual.

They finally reached a big road made of little stones. This is the road Sabina followed when going to school. They were told to run ahead of the woman into the moonless night. The cowardly ones were whipped, pinched and pushed forward. The brave ones ran and disappeared into the distant dark until women feared for their safety and shouted them back. Sabina was pinched from time to time by almost everyone. She sobbed and screamed. She ran into the darkness, but was ordered to run back and run forward again. She was forced to run on her toes and, at times, on all fours - on her legs and her hands together. When the women sensed that she was exhausted, and indeed out of breath, they stopped torturing her.

They reached an open field. Some cows, goats and sheep were tethered to trees. The girls and the women went past them silently. The cows lowed, and the sheep bleated. When the procession had gone far from them, the animals calmed down again. The vast field was decorated with yellow colour of scattered chrysanthemums. Short thick bushes stood like dinosaurs in the dark field. The moon slid out of jagged rifts of clouds again and changed the dinosaurs back into bushes. Sabina watched the sky and her predicament ended for a while.

After the open field, the procession entered into a thick forest whose trees had long branches and thick foliage. It was dark, and the women flashed their torches to light the dark corridors of foliage and dense woods. Sabina realized that it was colder here than it was in the open field. The procession went across a steep hill, below which snaked the river they had left behind. After half an hour of going round the hill, the women stopped. The girls held their breath.

"Now, we are about to reach the valley," a thin, tall, wild-eyed woman spoke. Sabina was familiar with her voice and seemed to know the red scarf - it was Lokolo-kolo. "You are supposed to behave! Be brave! Be focused and concentrate! Now observe silence as we descend!"

The women led the way down a steep descent that was surrounded by tall huge trees. The place was quiet and ghostly. Sabina looked around for a clue, but none was there. Her heart started beating faster. She was afraid of the cut. It was not her choice to have it. It was against her consent. She had pestered and pleaded with her parents to spare her the knife, but none could hear of it. Dowry had been paid and her marriage sealed. She thought about the cut and the thought of it made her shiver.

Valley of Death

When they reached the centre of the valley they met with several groups of girls. The groups, together with their women guardians, had come from other villages. There were now hundreds of them and the tall steep hills surrounded them like one huge house. Sabina noted that the little girls were all afraid and were shivering with terror. Some were younger than her, while others were as old as she was. They were clad in *lesos,* their teeth chattering and their small torsos rocking in the windless valley.

"Now, lie down, all of you!" one woman commanded. Those girls who hesitated, wondering whether to obey the command or not, were whipped and pushed down to the bare ground. They lay in a straight line. Sabina realized that the tall trees splashed down huge drops of water that made them wet. As she lay prone Sabina wondered what was going on around them.

As they lay down there, the girls' backs were splashed with cold water. A woman went round brushing their little backs with *rise,* a stinging, poisonous plant that made them wriggle in anguish and pain. The girls who were seen touching their backs to ease the itch were beaten thoroughly. It was against custom for any girl to touch her back no matter the amount of pain or itch on it. Sabina squirmed and felt the pain seethe up to her heart, then snake up to her throat, and enter her head. She closed her eyes and sobbed.

The crowd of women burst into a song. They also seemed to be dancing along with the song. The words in the song encouraged them to be brave as the ogre shaped them into women. Sabina listened to every word and her heart sank. Then shortly the voice of Lokolo-kolo was heard over their heads, saying: "now the time you have been waiting for has finally come!" She was heard greeting and welcoming into the valley a very prominent person. The personality was a lady going by her voice. Sabina heard this woman sharpening a piece of metal on a stone nearby. Sabina knew it was a knife; her body trembled. The exercise was about to begin.

As Sabina lay, near dead, on her stomach on that cold ground she heard a sharp scream that came from the first girl at the other end of the line.

"Stop biting me!" a voice shouted with a tone of urgency.

"Saucy girl, stop your hands, let the ogre eat you!" another voice added.

"Let go the ogre! Let go the ogre!" more voices screamed in unison.

The exercise had begun, no doubt. Sabina and the other girls had to be moulded into women. They had to be cast into nubile girls who would fetch enormous dowry for the village. They were expected to make their parents and the entire village proud.

As Sabina lay on that damp ground, she could hear rapturous applauses being made for the brave girls who had successfully been eaten by the ogre; she also heard jeers for the cowardly ones. The cheers and jeers filled the air, mixing with the women's song, producing a concoction of noise that sounded eerie and unearthly in Sabina's ears. It would be a matter of minutes before her turn came. Her numb fingers clutched at the undergrowth beside her head and she shut her eyes tight in fear. Her tiny body quivered and shook. Tears flowed freely and moistened the bare earth below. Her body became stiff, gripped with terror and horror. She held her breath and her heart almost stopped beating.

She was invaded with a thought: to run away, to run away and escape the cut. The cut, as she was taught at school, could have negative effects upon her health. It could also bring what she had told her mother: cervical cancer. What of the lump she had seen on her cousin's private organ? It was frighteningly huge. The cut could bring a similar growth on her *gento*. She could not wait to have all these effects on herself.

She decided to run away. But where was she to run to? What will her mother and father say? Her mother, who had been her mentor, will be heart-broken to hear of her escape. She will feel let down. The entire village would speak and gossip about her. She will be the talk of the village for so many generations to come. No, Sabina was not going to run away. She could not afford to let her parents down; she could not afford to let her friends down; she could not afford to let her relatives down; she could not afford to let the entire village down. It will be a shame!

Suddenly the girl, third from her, became a whirlwind of arms and legs and sharp raking teeth and fingernails.

"Throw your hands backwards!" a nervous murmur came.

"Hold her hands!" someone shouted.

"Put her legs apart! Her legs!" another anxious voice burst forth.

A fierce struggle ensued. Sabina listened to every word and to every action and, for a moment, she thought she was dreaming. She held her breath and stiffened her fingers on the ground, so tightly that she heard them snap. Her heart skipped and pounded beneath her tattered *leso*. The ground beneath her shook and swayed, crushed and crumbled and she seemed to fall through into the hollowness, screaming and shouting for help. No one came to her aid. No God was around. Neither was her mother. Ghostly drums seemed to beat in her head, clogging her ears and for a brief moment she was shut off from the world, from reality.

Suddenly the girl next to her burst into a scream, a sharp scream that broke the serenity of the valley. The women went mum and only whispers and breathing could be heard. Sabina shuddered, like a race horse before a race, yet also with a kind of fear. Sweat trickled down her nape, and she could feel it accumulating at the tip of her chin.

It was now Sabina's turn. It was her chance to become a woman. She had twice escaped the cruel knife that is meant to shape her into a woman. Now the time had come and she had no two ways out of it. Sabina was lifted up by the scruff of her neck, and as they did so, she closed her eyes tightly. Her little body was thrown on the initiation stone, a depressed ground whose floor was a flat rock, behind which stood a *mogumo* tree. Her hands were thrown back on to the tree. Her legs were spread apart.

"Sit properly, saucy girl!" a frail voice hissed. "Look up to the air!" the voice added. Sabina's head was tilted up by a hand. Silence invaded the valley.

Shortly afterwards Sabina felt a hand groping towards her organ. She winced; she brought her legs together. "Stop it!" a voice urged and pushed those tiny legs apart. Her legs started shaking. She cringed and shook with terror. When her legs had found peace, a hand again clandestinely crept below them, went up her thighs and reached for her *gento*. She winced; she fidgeted and moved her legs. "Stop playing with us, little girl!" a voice shouted and pushed the tiny legs apart once more. Silence ensued. Her breath came thickly. She waited, and there came the same hand again, creeping about her legs, going along her thighs, and finally reaching her organ. Sabina cringed and shouted: "Oh, no! Mama-a-a-a, where are you?"

"What?" a woman's voice came sharp, with a twinge of shock.

"Hold her, women!" voices shouted in unison.

They had sensed trouble with her. They had to ensure she was cut. More women were summoned to surround Sabina. With the reinforcement of women, the circumciser hoped to succeed this time round. She brought out her hand again, moved it along the tiny legs, up the boney thighs and reached the tiny organ. Caressed it gently. Then caressed it again. Sabina winced and moved her legs. She then shouted: "Oh no! Don't circumcise me!"

Shock wrinkled everyone's face. More reinforcement was built around her. She was threatened with dire consequences if she ever moved her legs again. The circumciser inserted her hand again, drove it gently up her thighs. She froze it there for a while, before finally reaching Sabina's organ. Sabina didn't wince, but tightened her eyes and tightened her legs and hand muscles.

"The bravery test is complete!" the circumciser whispered to other women. "She is now brave and ready." She turned herself round and picked up a whetting stone. She then took her traditional knife and ran it gently several times on the piece of stone, making an ear-renting and teeth-irritating sound that sent a cold terror into Sabina's heart. A violent trembling seized and shook Sabina, and she subsequently farted!

"Pheeeeeew!" the women exclaimed, pinching their noses.

"Bad manners!" one woman rebuked, and all of them burst into a delirious laughter.

"Don't be a coward, saucy girl!" another whispered.

"How can you break wind at such a reckoning hour of the ritual?" another wondered.

"Forgive her," another concluded. "It must have been just a slip of the wind."

After running the knife on the stone several times, the circumciser touched the blade with her fingers to gauge the degree of its sharpness. "It is now ready," she whispered to other women. She knelt between Sabina's thin legs and signalled to the other women to be ready for a song.

Sabina was trembling. She had waited for another touch of her thing, but the touch never came. Suddenly, now, being wielded in the air above her was that crude, cruel knife. That bloody metal came cutting through the darkness. It hovered above her like an eagle ready to grab and fly off. It came down, slashing through the chilling night. Before it could touch her organ, before it could turn her into a woman, Sabina burst into one loud scream that rent the still air of the valley. She then became a whirlwind of hands and legs. The circumciser closed her eyes to avoid being hurt and, in the confusion and panic, her knife dropped to the ground. As she was fumbling for it in the dark wet ground, Sabina, with the support of her right hand, lifted her torso up from the wet initiation stone, stepped on the piece of metal, and flew over the circumciser's back, bent low and crept under the withered knees, bony legs and near fleshless thighs of octogenarians.

The women were caught unawares. The octogenarians' feeble legs and poor judgment enabled Sabina to squeeze her little body through the over-flowing skirts and shawls and slip away. She could feel their withered hands, vein-lined arms and clammy fingers reaching for her heels, her back and the tip of her *leso*. The octogenarians were left sprawling on the bare earth, as Sabina fled from them, like a leaf from a storm, tripping, stumbling, falling on and rising from the uneven dark ground of the valley; and finally jumping over the hedgerow that guarded the valley.

"*Huyo! Huyo! Shika yeye!*" they shouted.

"Women run! Women run!" Shouts and cries reverberated through the dark forest.

By the time reality dawned on them, Sabina had disappeared into the dark night. They clutched their cheeks and could not believe their eyes. It had never happened before. Nothing like this!

A Hermit in the Forest

As she ran, Sabina jumped over a thick hedgerow and fell headlong onto the tall grass. She brought her little body up and started running over thick undergrowth. Her right foot got entangled in the undergrowth and she fell on the exuberant grass. Panting and perspiring, Sabina rose again and continued sprinting along, her heart beating like a roll of drums. She reached a thorny fence and squeezed her little frame through it, bruising her forehead, bare legs and arms. She managed to come out into an open field. The field motivated her to summon more energy; her legs went up and down, while her hands paddled hard through the air. Her breath came quickly; she was exhausted. She slowed down and dropped her body onto the ground in the middle of the field.

Breathless and gasping, Sabina looked back through the darkness and there was nobody chasing after her. Many miles away she could hear the cries and moaning of women in the valley. *"Uuuuuuiiiii!"* the cries rose and slowly died in the distant darkness; came up again, steadily, and died below the hills; intensified once again and slowly faded; and finally Sabina could not hear it any more.

The time was about three in the morning. The moon shone and lit the night. Sabina feared to continue with the journey for fear of wild animals. From where she was seated she could see light flickering inside a clump of dark woods at the end of the field. She stood up and peered keenly: a thatched hut surrounded by dense woods and thick foliage. Sabina held her breath and stealthily walked towards it. She stood behind a line of tall trees and peered keenly. No one was in sight. She wanted to go into the cleared space outside the hut, but feared. Her heart beat fast; a thought urged her to go, while a remote feeling held her back. She stood still, transfixed on the spot, looking blankly. She finally decided to try it out. She squeezed through the dense woods and came to the space outside the hut.

The lone hut was made of timber and thatch grass. It was also painted in white colour. The door and a small window were both made of wood. Sabina tip-toed towards the wall. She stood beside the window and sneaked a look through its cracks. Inside the hut was a tiny tin-lamp on a small rickety table. Beside it was a young boy kneeling on the earthen floor. Sabina saw his hands rising and clasping at his chest. His head bowed down. The boy was praying. Why was he praying? Sabina wondered. Why was he up so early? Why was he living alone in this lonely hut far away from other people? Sabina turned her head onto the right and saw in the dark night a cross of wood stuck on a mound of soil. It was a fresh grave. Maybe it was the boy's parents who had died and he was left alone as an orphan. Sabina stole a look through the cracks again and the boy was still kneeling, his hands tightly locked into each other on his chest. She sympathized with him. She wanted to knock on the door and get in and talk to him, but feared in case he could be a sorcerer. She peered again and the boy's body was still frozen in the same position.

Sabina suddenly coughed. "Oh, my!' she exclaimed and cringed. The cough startled the boy and he suddenly scrambled to his feet. Sabina feared and sprang onto her feet and flew away towards the dark woods. As she squeezed through the forest, she heard a voice behind her: "Who are you? Don't run away! Come back! Come back!" It was the boy calling. Thinking the boy was pursuing her, Sabina, in confusion and dread, crept through the woods and ran towards the river. She found a footpath that snaked along the river's edge. She followed it. She quickly looked back at the small hut and gasped. No one was chasing after her. She slowed down and took in a deep breath and let it out noisily. She hoped to find another hut, or place, where she could lay her head for the remaining part of the night. She felt exhausted, hungry and thirsty. She longed for water, for food, for a bed and for a human being. She laboured on drunkenly and dreamily.

After a long trek Sabina realized that the footpath was leading to a very dark and dense forest. She feared wild animals would eat her. She stopped. She needed to cross the river and look for life on the other side. She walked over tall grass and reached near the bank. The surface of the water looked silvery from the reflection of the moon. The river swirled and heaved. She moved closer to test the depth of the water near the bank with her right leg. She knelt and inserted the foot into the waters. Oops! by bad luck her left knee lost balance and she plunged into the raging water.

"Wo-o-o-o-o !" She shouted. "Wo-o-o-o-o ! Help! Help!"

The waves swept her along as she paddled her hands and kicked her legs. She threw her head up and continued slapping the waters with her hands. She raised her head again and successfully reached the bank on the other side of the river. She clutched the grass on the bank and lifted her torso up the mound of soil. She was wet and shivered in the darkness. She wrung the helm of her *leso.* Suddenly she heard a noise. She held her breath and listened. The sound came again. It was louder this time. She moved from the river bank and walked up the farm of maize. When she was about to come out in a clearing, an animal suddenly ran towards her. She quickly moved out of the way and it flew past. Before long the same animal ran back and directed its teeth at her. "Wow!" Sabina screamed and jumped aside. The animal was scared by the scream and ran away. It was a young hyena.

Her heart beat rapidly. She hurried out of the maize farm and reached a footpath that ran through a forest. It was dark and the moon hid her face behind a rift of clouds. Suddenly she heard a crow, and a series of barking followed by croaking sounds. She knew she had reached a place where people lived. Below the hills were men shouting at their oxen as they ploughed their farm. It was now around four in the morning. The human sounds cheered her heart up and made her walk quickly and confidently. Her *leso* was still wet and water dripped from it, and from time to time she would gather its hems and wring it dry.

Before long she was in a glade. A small hut stood in the centre of the clearing. The light she had seen earlier was actually coming from the lamp inside this hut. She tiptoed towards the hut. She stood at the door that was made of sticks and smeared with cow dung. She stood quietly before it and listened. A grinding sound came from inside. She bent and, through a gap on the lower part of the door, took a quick peek inside. She saw a slender woman squatting, grinding millet on a stone. She was so thin that Sabina thought she could be a witch. Sabina was seized by fright. Witches are normally thin and bony, she thought. The woman was also suspect since she lived alone, away from the main village. Sabina panicked. She wanted to run away and leave that place.

Instead of running away Sabina found herself hesitating. Maybe she was a kind of person who could offer her something to eat. She could also provide her with a dry *leso* to change. These prospects urged Sabina to knock on the door and call upon the lady. But before she could do so, something held her back. She thought that the act could plunge her into trouble. Suppose the woman is a cannibal, she thought. She had heard of women who killed other people and ate their flesh and drank their blood. If the woman turned out to be dangerous, Sabina, being young and weak, might not be able to resist or fight her back. The old woman could call upon her accomplices and, together, they will slaughter Sabina, remove her heart and chop off her liver and tongue. These, it was said, were the parts needed by witches and cannibals. They believed the organs could be used to make one rich and successful. The possibility of this happening sent a shudder down her back.

While Sabina's mind wandered, the door suddenly opened! She froze on the spot, tongue-tied. A crumpled figure, with piercing eyes, stood motionless in the door-way. Sabina was about to take off, but clammy fingers clawed her hand. Sabina shook with shock. She wanted to shout for help, but her mouth could not open. She looked up at the skeleton of a woman before her, and she shivered.

"Who are you?" the emaciated figure asked. Her voice was not harsh. Neither did it sound mysterious like that one of a witch. The old woman was friendly. Sabina composed herself and looked at her in the face.

"I am Sabina," she said and trembled.

"Come in," the woman said and detached her clammy hand from Sabina's and led the way in. Sabina hesitated. "Come in, don't fear," the old woman reassured her, kindness in her voice. "Come and tell me what brings you here in this wee hour of dawn."

"I was just —," Sabina started speaking and got stuck. What brought her here at such wee hours of dawn? How did she come to find this hut? Sabina's mind went blank. She found herself trundling into the hut without resistance.

"Have a seat," the old woman offered, pointing to the three-legged stool in the middle of the hut. She squatted before the grinding stone and resumed her work. The woman's torso moved forward and backward. She took a break from time to time to add more millet onto the stone and resumed her movement. Her face was thin and her jaws jutted out like a cliff of a rock. Her hair was thick sisal and this scared Sabina. Sabina sat trembling, partly because of the cold and partly due to fear. The woman, realizing Sabina was wet, stood up and went to the corner of the hut and ransacked a huge basket. She came back with a red *leso* and handed it to Sabina.

"Remove that wet *leso* and put on this dry one," the old woman said, her voice warm and friendly.

"Thank you," Sabina uttered, standing up.

She put on the dry *leso* and pulled the wet one below it. The woman looked up and narrowed her eyelids into slits. "You should have removed the wet one first before putting on the dry one," she barked.

Sabina nervously stammered something incoherently. She placed the wet *leso* onto the table next to her. The woman kept pushing the grinding-stone back and forth. After some time she stood up. "I have finished this daunting work," she stated. She sat on a three-legged stool next to Sabina and looked into Sabina's face. The woman then asked: "Now tell me, what brings you this way?"

"They wanted…" Sabina started. "They wanted to cut me!" she said and dropped her head to stifle a sob.

"Cut you? How?"

"They wanted to circumcise me," Sabina said in a moaning voice.

"Oh, they wanted to circumcise you?"

"Yes, but I ran away," Sabina said and cupped her chin in the palm of her right hand.

"You ran away?" the old lady asked and scanned Sabina's face. "Where was the cutting taking place?"

"In the valley over there!" Sabina pointed towards the direction of the valley.

"Oh, The Valley of Death, that is how we call it," the old lady expressed. "So what made you decide to run away?" Sabina was now getting suspicious. She thought the woman might hold her hostage and call for her parents and the women to take her back to the valley to get the cut. She decided that she was not going to tell her everything she wanted to know. "So what made you run away?"

"Nothing?"

"Nothing? What do you mean?" the old lady inquired, astonished. "Had they lined you up for the cut, or did you run away before reaching the Valley of Death?"

"Nothing," Sabina replied.

"Nothing?" the woman asked, scanning her from toe to head. She then thought the girl was daft or simply shy. She decided to make her feel free with her. "What do you want to eat?" she changed the subject. Sabina was hungry and really wanted something to eat. She looked up and said: "Food, drink, fruit, anything."

The old lady stood up and headed towards the fireplace at the corner of the hut. "Let me prepare for you porridge, then I will cook for you some *ugali,*" she said, bending down to make fire. Sabina was very happy and was already salivating. "I know you are hungry, considering the fact that you have walked in the dark all the way from the Valley of Death."

The woman sang an old tune while she prepared the porridge. Sabina listened to the tune and it was sweet. She wanted to ask about the meaning of the song, but decided not to. She had been rude to her by behaving the way she did. She wished she could now provide answers to the questions the old woman had asked. The woman continued singing beside the fire, amid the noise of boiling water and flour.

The woman finished preparing porridge and placed a cup on the table before Sabina. She then poured hot porridge into it. Sabina licked her lips and trembled at the prospect of drinking it. She lifted the cup to the mouth and cringed when it touched her lips. She placed it back on the table and looked at the emaciated figure before her.

"Is it hot?" the figure asked.

"Yes."

"Wait for it to cool down," the old woman advised.

Sabina looked at the woman and thought she was not bad after all. She could tell her everything and maybe seek her advice. She had displayed kindness by making her warm and giving her something to eat.

"Why do you live alone here, grandma?" Sabina started.

"Now that is the question," the old lady intoned. "That is the question." She then moved her three-legged stool near Sabina. "I am here for a reason," she explained, stared at the empty wall opposite and her mind seemed to have frozen in space. She then suddenly turned her head towards Sabina and said: "The story is a long one," she said and stopped. She then continued: "But quite relevant to your present predicament."

"Tell me, grandma," Sabina craved for the story.

"Our people—," she began, and suddenly sighed. She closed her eyes tightly and bent her head. She then placed her right hand on her chest. The old woman gasped, blew her nose, then wiped tears from her eyes. Sabina was astonished. "My daughter," she sobbed. Sabina placed her cup on the table, and listened, her mouth gaping. "Our people are not kind, they are not considerate."

"Yes, grandma," Sabina listened, empathy ringing in her voice.

"They banished me from the village," the woman explained and broke down into tears.

"Banished you? Why, grandma?"

"Because of the same reason that you are here for," she said, and wiped tears from her eyes. She bent down and placed her chin in the palms of her hands and seemed to close her eyes. She appeared to have gone far into the distant past, searching in her mind's store for pieces of the story she wanted to narrate. "It started when my husband discovered that I was not circumcised," she narrated. Sabina adjusted her small body on the stool and paid attention. "I made it worse when I spared my daughters from the cut."

"Oh, grandma!" Sabina exclaimed. She ran her eyes over the old woman's bony features and she was filled with compassion.

"My husband and the whole village ganged up against me and my daughters," the old lady explained and pulled mucus up her nostrils.

"What did they do?"

"They expelled us from the village," she said. "They said we were a disgrace to the village. They called us all imaginable nick names. The village woke up one morning and drove me and my daughters out. We had no place to go. We came down to this forest to live. We lived in the caves for three months. God helped us to construct this hut."

"So where are your daughters?"

"Oh, my daughters are all married," the woman said, smiling. "They are three; they now have children."

"They are still not cut?"

"Oh, no!" the old lady cried. "They will not be cut and will not cut their daughters when they grow up." Sabina nodded her head. "They are determined to keep their line of generations knife-free."

"Grandma, I am surprisingly amazed to learn that you are not cut," Sabina was delighted.

"Come on, drink your porridge," she teased Sabina and smiled. "It is sweeter when hot."

"Do you intend to go back to your village?" Sabina asked.

"I sometimes visit. But that is only once in a blue moon."

"They don't harm you in any ways?

"Oh no. They only refer to me as a hermit. My name has come to be 'hermit'."

"They do not harm you at all?"

"Oh no, so long as I don't live among them, they have no business with me."

"What will happen if you live among them?"

"They will circumcise me forcibly."

"Even at your advanced age?"

"Yes, they will. They will cut you by force, especially during the time of giving birth. And if you die before they cut you, they will do so on your corpse, sing songs and carry out all the rituals. They trust tradition so much."

"Oh, my!" Sabina exclaimed.

"Now, you have done a great thing to run away from the cut," the old lady congratulated her. "You have done yourself justice. Never regret what you have done. Luckily enough, you have landed on safe arms!"

"I am really glad, grandma, to be here, to have found you," Sabina said and sipped from her cup.

"Your good angel guided you here, I am sure," she said and smiled, her banana-stained teeth grimacing in the dim light.

"Now, grandma, what do I do?"

"Now that is the question," the old lady said and nodded. "What to do? You have already done it, my granddaughter!" she said. "You have now become part of this knife-free generation that we are building."

"What do you advise me?" Sabina insisted.

"First, do you want to go back to the village, or you want to stay with me here?" the old lady asked.

"Well, I feel I must go back to my mother," Sabina proposed.

"Well, that is alright. But you will need to live with me here for a week. After a week the season for the cutting will be long gone and you will be safe back there."

"I know. It will be another year before another season comes."

"That is right," the old woman intoned. "There are three incidences when they can possibly cut you: During the cutting season like now. Or when one is giving birth. And also when you are dead. None of these are a risk to you as per now."

"What will I do when the next season comes?"

"Do not worry. There will be an answer by then," the old woman said.

"I will come to live with you here long before the season starts," Sabina said.

"Yes that is obvious. But wait—" the old woman's face wrinkled. "You know your case is different. You are *enkuri,* a crier. Once you run away from the initiation stone, or resist the cut, as you did, you become *enkuri.* In my case I never reached the initiation stone as you did. There is a penalty for that if you go back to the village. The ultimatum for it is death, slaughter of goats and what not." She said and cupped her chin in her palm.

"Well, I am not afraid," Sabina said. "I just want to go back. Whatever happens let it happen." Sabina said and the old woman peered at her with astonishment.

"Well, you want to go back regardless of whatever happens?" the old woman asked, her eyes wide open.

"Yes, if they kill me, let them,"

"After all, we should confront this monster head on," the old lady said and bit her low lip. "For how long shall we fear taking this vice by the horns?"

"I want to belief that nothing will happen," Sabina said.

"Nothing might happen. The village is changing and it better change"

"We are the ones to change it" Sabina added.

"Yes, by walking into the lion's den."

Outside the sun had sent its rays over the woods and the forest was warm. Sabina looked out and was cheerful. A new day had come. She recalled the events of the previous night and the dramatic escape from the knife. The night journey was dangerous, she thought. She was lucky to be alive. She risked wild animals, witches, raging rivers and rapists.

The old woman stood beside her rumpled bed and put on a pullover and old gumboots. "Now we can walk around and I will show you my farm," she said. Sabina, feeling warm and happy, stood up at once and led the way out.

"You don't use a padlock here, grandma?"

"Oh, no. There is nobody who can open the door. We don't have thieves or bad people here. All the people living by the river are friendly and will come to your help when you are in trouble."

The sun had lightened all the spaces in the forest. The river was very close by. Sabina looked around and thought the place was nice. The night before the place appeared a ghostly and witch-invested area. Now, during the day, she found it lovely. The rippling of the water sent in a sweet sound that soothed her mind. The tall trees provided a shed that was good for reading and studying. Sabina was pleased she was going to live here for the next one week.

In a Trance!

The homestead was desolate. Silence hovered over the huts like a shroud. Thin music spilled from a one-stringed instrument being played under a tree by a well-known old man, *Mzee* Onduche. He was reputed for playing dirges at funerals. Birds floated lazily in the air, making shrill sounds that moaned and screamed. The owl flew in and perched itself on a tall tree on the hedgerow and hooted; its echo reverberated against the huts and tall trees in the compound and it sounded grave and solemn.

The old man of the homestead sat alone, sad. *Enkuri!* he thought. His daughter was *enkuri,* a crier. In addition to being *enkuri* she also escaped and didn't receive the cut. She reneged on all the ritual procedures.

The old man fell into a trance and explored the interiors of his being. He had walked through the dark corridors of his life and had come very close to the end where light shone, but darkness snapped it away. He had stared at a fortune, but it suddenly went down the drain. He had become very close to being a man, but suddenly things changed and he became worse than *enana,* a child.

The fifty plus heads of cattle will be taken away by his would-have-been son in-law in a dramatic manner that had never happened in the village. He will remain as poor as he was before. People will talk mockingly about him and his family. Gossip will do the rounds in the village. He will not sit among men and drink or eat in the village functions. The shame of Sabina's action weighed heavily upon his heart. He thought he had become a total man, but little did he know he had spiralled into *enana*. He had swiftly and easily climbed up to the top-most rung on the village ladder, only to come tumbling down to the ground. Now, as he lay sprawled on the grass, he looked up to the top of the ladder and saw how far he had climbed, or was to climb, had Sabina endured the pain at the initiation stone. Had she accepted the ogre, he could be so many miles up above his fellow men. He could be planning to marry his second wife by now. He could also be planning to be called *sokoro,* grandpa, a senior title in the village. He could also have taken the title of *omoruoti,* a wise elderly man. His status and the new titles - as a grandpa and as a wise elderly man - could have endeared him well in the village. What a shame!

The old man suddenly stood and peered at the herd of cattle. Tomorrow, he thought, they will be driven away, shame was worse than death. The devil of a daughter had caused all this misery and torture in his heart. As he stood peering at the herd, he cursed the day he married Sabina's mother and the day the little devil was conceived in her womb. It was worse than not having had a daughter at all.

A Ghost?

By mid-day the vast field was filled with people. It was a day for appeasing *enkuri,* the curse of crying. Sabina's actions at the initiation stone had to be appeased. The sin had to be atoned. Seven bulls were slaughtered. Beer and *ugali* were prepared and served. *Ribuogore,* traditional beer, was also served in five big pots: one pot for the elderly men, another for the aged women, the third for young people, the fourth for relatives and the last one for village hunters. People drank and ate silently as a way of cleansing the curse of *enkuri.* It was a solemn occasion and the first in the history of the village.

In the middle of this ritual, the burly, bald-headed, pot-bellied old man arrived with his entourage. They were given a special place to sit under a *mogumo* tree that stood near the main hut in the homestead.

Pa Sabina sat among the elderly men who consoled and spoke words of insight to him. He was aggrieved and, in many ways, bereaved. Ma Sabina, on the other hand, sat among the senior women. These were women reputed for their great wisdom and knowledge.

As the ceremony was underway, a ten-year old boy burst into the centre of the field, panting. "Sabina! Sabina!" he shouted. "Sabina there! Look there!" he said, pointing towards the gate. People were startled and peered into the distance. A young girl was walking towards them. True, it was Sabina.

"Ghost! Ghost! Kill! Kill" young men shouted as they sprung up, weapons in hand.

"She brings bad omen to our village!" one man shouted on top of his voice.

"She is *enkuri!* She must be killed!" all the young men bellowed in unison.

"Kill her to safe the village!" one old man advised, as the young men, openly agitated, appeared ready to maim the little girl.

People shouted. The noise level rose. Young women held their breaths. The elderly placed their hands on their chests. Grandmas clutched their cheeks. Children screamed and held tightly onto their mothers' breasts. Sabina walked on, undeterred. Soon, she was close by.

"Do not kill me!" Sabina cried out and raised her hands.

"Kill! Kill! Kill!" the men shouted

"A curse! A curse upon our village!"

"Do not kill me!" Sabina's voice came tenderly, shivering. "I have done no wrong."

"Kill to safe this village!" more voices surfaced.

"I have wronged no one!" Sabina's tender voice came again as she walked to the front of the crowd.

Pa Sabina, upon sighting his daughter, fainted and dropped down on the grass. What a shame! People were seen helping him up and untying his tight clothes. Others were fanning him using their own coats and pullovers. Later he was carried away to his hut to come to.

"Kill! Kill! Kill!" voices rose.

Suddenly Ma Sabina thrust forward towards her daughter. She grabbed Sabina by the torso, breaking down beside her. Ma Sabina shed tears uncontrollably. "My lovely daughter!" she sobbed. "Do not kill my daughter!" she pleaded and raised his hand to the men. "Do not strike! She has done no wrong!" she screamed. "She has wronged no one!" People watched in astonishment.

Young men held their spears. The old men held their mouths agape, not knowing what advice to give next. Suddenly a village elder came to the front. He looked at the crowd, tongue-tied. The crowd gaped at him.

"Speak, the wise one! Speak! All wisdom is yours!" people cheered him on as they charged and jostled in great confusion. The village elder could not find his words. "Speak! The wise one! Speak!" people urged him on. He remained tongue-tied. All that came out of his mouth was not words. Instead, tears of compassion welled up in his eyes and flowed freely down his cheeks. He gasped and choked, wiping his face.

"Speak old man!" people shouted as they surrounded Sabina.

"Kill! Kill! Kill!" a voice rose.

"Speak the wise one!" young men shouted, putting their spears on the ready. The old man finally found a word to say. He uttered, thus: "Wait!" He then bent down and shook his head in dismay.

"Old man, give us direction!"

"Tell us to kill!"

"Please spare my daughter!" Ma Sabina pleaded, sobbing.

"A curse! A curse!" the young men bellowed

"Give us direction!"

"You are the wise one!" the young men urged him on.

"Please! Please!" Ma Sabina cried, cuddling her daughter.

The village elder wiped his eyes and explored the crowd. Then, parting his lips, he uttered: "Spare the life of this little one! I am pleading to you! Spare her!" People shook their heads and uttered cursing words at the old man.

Four of these men were seen leaving the scene in protest. "Our cultural fabric is soiled," they shouted towards the crowd as they walked out of the gate. "The wise ones have turned against us!" they declared. Those left behind were confused and did not know how to react. Murmurs ensued.

Undeterred, the elder continued with his speech: "It is time we looked keenly into the culture that we embrace." With this, the people looked at one another, bewildered. "It is time we examined the pros and cons of what we think is important to us," he said. The crowd quietened. Most young men held back their spears.

Suddenly, there appeared from a distance, an old lady. She was dressed in a black *leso.* Attention now shifted to her, giving Sabina and her mother some momentary reprieve as people looked in her direction. She looked familiar. She was the hermit, who had been banished from the community and was living by the riverside. She walked on and when she came closer, people shouted: "Another curse! The hermit! Curse! Kill!" Young people ran up to her and roughed her up.

"Please do not kill me!" the hermit pleaded, raising her hands up.

"Do not kill her either," the village elder turned to tell them. "Do not touch her!' he commanded with authority. "Wait!" he added.

"Listen! Listen everyone!" a compassionate voice came from the crowd. It was Lokolo-kolo, a woman who was known and respected for her foresight and wisdom. She was seen jostling through the people, hurrying and making her way to the front of the crowd. "No-o-o-o-o-! Wait" she commanded, waving her hand towards the young men. The young people, detecting the seriousness in her voice, put their spears on hold. The hermit walked straight to the front of the crowd as well. She held Sabina's hand as she burst into a loud sob. The trio embraced one another as they wailed, holding onto one another's hands.

"My daughter," Ma Sabina sobbed.

"Our people!" Lokolo-kolo spoke.

"Ye-e-e-s," the crowd responded with enthusiasm.

"The wise old one! Speak!" the men shouted.

"The wise one! Give direction!" the old men finally wanted a verdict.

"Give us a word of wisdom!" women requested.

Lokolo-kolo continued: "Our culture…" she said and stopped amid cheers, applause and anxiety. She explored the crowd and waved her hand. Silenced, the crowd waited.

"Speak! The wise one," women motivated her.

"Tell us to strike now! Now!" a flurry of voices came out loud.

Lokolo-kolo continued when the noise subsided: "What I am saying is that our culture comes first."

"Yes, our culture comes first! Speak! Let us strike!" the young people were enraged.

"Our culture comes first," she repeated. "One without a culture has no identity and is as good as dead."

"The wise one, you are right!" people shouted

"These two are dead!" the crowd went hysterical

"Kill them!" the old men urged.

"Without culture, you are an alienated individual" Lokolo-kolo continued. "But, but, but, but, but…"

"But we kill!"

"But, we banish them!"

"But we burn them alive!"

"But, we need to be thoughtful," Lokolo-kolo stated and people quietened. "We need to be intelligent. We need to question every aspect of our culture." There was silence. The young men clutched their spears fiercely. "We need to be wise. Wisdom calls for wise decisions and wise judgements. We need to act soberly, with intelligence and understanding." The young men impatiently shook their spears. The women sighed. The old men shook their heads. "This little girl," Lokolo-kolo added, turning towards Sabina. "And this old lady whom we banished years ago…" she said and suddenly stopped. She covered her face with the palms of her hands. She gasped and shook. She convulsed. She was sobbing. She bit her low lip with her teeth and shivered amid tears. People lowered their heads in dismay. Feelings of empathy ate into the hearts and minds of many of those present. They shook their heads and finally spears fell from the young men's hands.

"This is a different era we live in," she continued after wiping her eyes. "A different age. Women are respected more than before. Their rights, yes, their rights, are respected and upheld more than they were before." People listened, some amazed and others obviously confused.

Suddenly, three middle-aged men were seen pushing through the crowd. With their heads bowed in remorse, they walked to the front of the crowd and broke down beside Sabina, her mother and the hermit. The three men clenched their teeth in pity.

"This era is different from the old days," Lokolo-kolo continued amid air of regret and grief. "Things have changed," Lokolo-kolo stopped and explored the crowd. They were restless and pain was written all over their faces. "We used to get water from the river, now we get it from the tap; we used to walk on foot, now we board *matatus*; we used to fight using arrows, now we fight using guns. How things have changed!" She paused! The crowd was attentive.

"If we used to circumcise, it does not mean we can continue doing so. Let us give this young girl and the old lady whom we banished, a chance to live their lives. If they want to remain dirty as they are, let them. If they want to endure the scorn of being called *egesagane,* let them. If they want to undergo the cut later, let them. Give them a chance to live their own lives." The people took in a deep breath and let it out noisily. Some nodded their heads gently in agreement with Lokolo-kolo's sentiments; others mumbled as if in defeat given the sentiment of the majority. Two young people and one old man were seen walking away from the crowd as a sign of protest.

"You have soiled the garment of our cultural fabric," a voice came from the protesting group, as they walked past the gate. The rest of the crowd who remained listening to Lokolo-kolo showed a sign of indecisiveness and remained mumbling to themselves.

"Now, for Sabina, let her live with her parents and continue with schooling. We all shall respect her status and support her education. For the old woman here, let her come back home and live among us. We should promise that we shall respect them and give them a chance to live among us." She stopped and looked at the few people who were still present. Their sentiment appeared non-committal. Everyone looked at each other. Then slowly, a murmur started amid the small crowd. People started discussing and chattering.

"This decision is unwise," one man was heard saying.

"We have really tampered with our culture," another added.

"Lokolo-kolo has really gone insane!" A whisper came.

More men were seen walking away in protest. They left the crowd and walked towards and past the gate. Only a handful of people remained behind to listen to Lokolo-kolo.

"With us we agree with what you have said!" one old man said.

"Yes, we agree!" another old man added.

"We shall respect them!" an old woman's voice came.

"Let them live their own life!" a few of the remaining young people finally uttered and raised their spears to the air as a sign of surrender.

"Let Sabina go to School!" one female voice added.

"We shall support her education!" a male voice emerged.

"They are our people, we cannot throw them away!" more voices came.

Sabina, her mother and the old hermit were seen wiping tears. The men and women who were present joined them to console them. Smiles were seen all over many people's faces. Sabina was hugged and young girls and women surrounded her, each one wanting to talk to her. The old hermit was delighted and wore a broad smile on her face. She went round to shake everyone's hands. Women patted her on the back telling her, "Come back! Come home grandma!"

The few young men who stayed behind carried Sabina on their shoulders as a sign of acceptance. They walked round the field as Sabina perched on their shoulders. Suddenly they burst into a song and started to dance. The village drummer, on hearing the song, ran from his hut and started beating his drum. They sang Sabina's name and, at times, uttered the hermit's name and at other times, alluded to Lokolo-kolo's wisdom. Those who were present saw this and marvelled. Some decided to run after the now joyous crowd and joined in the dance and the party became big. Others who had gone away in protest watched from behind the fences and gaped. A few squeezed through the fence and came back to the field and after moments of indecisiveness, ran after the crowd and joined in the dance and song. The old men who had rebelliously walked away in protest were seen coming back to the homestead. Later on, they too joined the dancing party.

Pa Sabina, who had fainted earlier, emerged from his hut. He appeared astonished with the development. He watched the ceremony with mixed reaction. At first he sneered and then later a smile built on his lower lip. His face finally brightened. He nervously clutched his walking stick and shook his head with delight. Despite the disappointments, he was glad that his daughter's live had been spared.

The people in the field clapped their hands and cheered the dancers on. Sabina waved her hands to the crowd and to those who had come back to the field as she perched on the men's shoulders. She had turned into a heroine. What a turn of events! What a change of heart! Who could believe this could happen in this village?

Glossary of Terms

Eee	yes
Egesagane	an uncircumcised girl
Egesagane eke	you, uncircumcised lass
Egesanda	calabash
Ekee	a traditional twig plate in which ugali is served
Enana	small child
Enkuri	A girl who cries/screams (a coward) during the cut. Such a girl is deemed a curse to the community.
Gento	thing, refering to 'clitoris'
Huyo! Huyo! Shika yeye!	Gather together and we get hold of her
Kegori	age-set or age mate
Leso	a shawl
Ma	Mother
Magokoro	grandmother
Matatu	passenger vehicle
Mzee	old man; an elder
Oiye-e--e-e-e-e!	chant of victory, hurrah!
Omogumo	an indigenous tree known for its resilience
Omong'ina	old woman
Omoruoti	village elder; a wise elderly man
Pa	Father
Ribuogore	tradiional brew

Rise	stinging nettle; stinging plant used to test girls' bravery in the Abagusii community before they undergo circumcision
Shuka	a type of shawl; not exactly the same as a *leso*
Sufuria	cooking pot made of aluminium
Titi	breast, but it also refers to a girl
Ugali	corn meal or millet meal